Of MONSTERS
and MADNESS

JESSICA VERDAY

EGMONT USA

New York

EGMONT

We bring stories to life

First published by Egmont USA, 2014
443 Park Avenue South, Suite 806
New York, NY 10016

1 3 5 7 9 8 6 4 2

www.egmontusa.com
www.jessicaverday.com

Library of Congress Cataloging-in-Publication Data
Verday, Jessica.
Of monsters and madness / by Jessica Verday.
pages cm
Summary: In 1820s Philadelphia, a girl finds herself in the midst of a rash
of gruesome murders in which her father and his alluring assistant
might be implicated.
ISBN 978-1-60684-463-2 (hardcover) -- ISBN 978-1-60684-464-9 (eBook)
[1. Murder--Fiction. 2. Philadelphia (Pa.)--History--19th century--Fiction.
3. Horror stories.] I. Title.
PZ7.V5828Of 2014
[Fic]--dc23
2014003140

Book design by Michelle Gengaro-Kokmen

Printed in the United States of America

For Alison — because it was your first
(and I know I'm biased, but I think it's your best) acquisition

It was many and many a year ago,

    In a kingdom by the sea,

That a maiden there lived whom you may know

    By the name of Annabel Lee . . .

— **"Annabel Lee" by Edgar Allan Poe**

Preface

My breath is quick. It abandons me, then rushes back so fiercely I fear I'm going to faint. The horrors—such horrors!—lie before me.

Blood is everywhere. Splashed on the walls and spilled across the floor. The scent, heavy upon the air, is like a fog that rises up early in the morning. Loops of glistening flesh are strung out upon a table, and in the middle of it all is a single lock of hair. Dark. Curled. Obscene in its loveliness amongst such carnage. I cannot comprehend that such a horrible act has been committed upon someone, and I close my eyes to say a silent prayer for their soul.

I've been witness to grim scenes as Mother's assistant, but nothing could prepare me for this. Only moments ago, this poor person was alive. And now . . .

A sound comes from behind me. I whirl around, and Edgar steps out of the shadows. "Do you like it?" he purrs. "The small intestine stretches quite far. It is remarkable."

"You did this?"

At his nod, I put one hand up to cover my mouth. Bile rises in the back of my throat and nausea threatens to overcome me. "Why . . . ?"

"To show you that I keep my word. If you deny my request, this will be Cook next. Carved upon my table like a Christmas ham. Or perhaps Johanna."

I take a step back and stumble. "I tried to find Father . . . to speak with him. . . . But he's gone out of town and has not yet returned."

Voices come from outside the room, and Edgar springs into action, pushing the door shut behind me, and shoving me backward. Curling his fingers into the collar of my cloak, he holds me up against the wall. My feet barely brush the floor.

"It's my best work yet," Edgar says. "Although rather messy." His voice, low in my ear, is taunting. "Don't you think?"

My heart thumps, and I silently beg him to let me go. To erase this horror from my mad, feverish brain. To let this torment finally come to an end.

His leg is pressed against mine and I feel the heat of his body singeing me through my dress. He pulls back to study me, cocking his head to one side, and I do what I should have done from the moment he first laid his hands upon me—I struggle.

But Edgar holds me tight. He dips his head, and his mouth is dangerously close to my throat. He pushes aside my scarf and I cry out.

And then, suddenly, he lets me go.

Blindly, I stumble away from him. With one hand against the wall, I feel my way toward the door. If I can only be free of this room, away from this house, I know I will be safe.

"Annabel," he calls out, and something in his voice gives me pause. "Do not forget your promise."

One

PHILADELPHIA, 1826

The carriage is late. My dress is torn. And the rumbling clouds overhead threaten a storm at any moment. Glancing anxiously at the gathering darkness, I pull the edges of my linen scarf closer around my neck. Although the dress I'm wearing is new, the scarf is old. A family heirloom passed down from Mother. I never take it off.

Shifting upon the surface of my steamer trunk, I huddle closer to the lone gas lamp casting a dim glow around me. The ship from Siam docked earlier in the day. I am the last remaining passenger. The letter I received said I would be met here by my father, but now doubt starts to creep in around the edges of my mind. *What if I've been forgotten? What will I do if no one comes?*

Nearby, two men barter, and I turn to watch their exchange. Their skin isn't darkened by the sun and their faces are not split with easy smiles like the people I am used to. Instead, these men's faces are pale and drawn. They are in such a hurry to go about their business with no signs of joy in their transaction. Everything is so black and bleak here in Philadelphia.

Bits of dirty straw and discarded fish heads litter the ground, and the air is ripe with soot-stained clouds and spray from the choppy sea waters. Wrinkled fishermen traverse the edges of the dock, tying up their vessels for the night as a small child runs amongst them, offering his services. They ignore him and he turns away, searching for another way to pay for his evening meal.

One of the fishermen drops a newspaper beside me and I bend down to pick it up. The headline reads: MURDER AT RITTENHOUSE SQUARE. POLICE FIND GRISLY SCENE OF DISMEMBERMENT.

My heart beats loudly in my ears. *This is to be my*

new home? A place of murder and death?

Suddenly, a tiny girl wearing dark skirts and a matching cloak appears in front of me and curtsies deeply. She is pale skinned, with a plait of red hair tied neatly to one side. In her hand is a piece of paper. She looks at it, and says, "Are you Miss Annabel Lee?"

"I am."

"Begging yer pardon for being so late. The horse threw a shoe an' it had to be replaced." She stands from her curtsy and bobs her head. "I'm Maddy, miss. Here to take you back to the house."

I smile and bow to her. "I was expecting my father to meet me."

"He was unavailable." She glances around. "Is there only one of you? We thought there would be two."

"My mother . . ." My voice breaks. Her death is still so fresh in my mind. The ache of losing her was like having my heart split in two, with one of the pieces lost forever. "She died a month before I received the letter informing me that passage had been booked to Philadelphia for us both. I have her unused ticket in my valise." I gesture to the small bag sitting at my feet.

Maddy's expression briefly changes to pity, but then

it's gone and she reaches for my valise. "I'll take this, an' Thomas, our footman, will see to yer trunk. Come with me. The carriage is this way."

Tucking the newspaper into the side of my valise, I hand it over to her and grasp my skirts firmly, trying not to step on any of the fish heads. The silk is heavy between my fingertips, and I long for the light cotton trousers and shirt I have packed away in my trunk. I can barely move in this ill-fitting garment. The only reason I'm wearing it is because it was sent to me along with the ship fare. I had put the gown on as soon as the ship came to shore, wanting to look my best for Father.

"Stay close." My companion turns around again, eyeing a thin man who is lingering in the shadows. She leads me down the dock and I can see a large carriage with even larger horses waiting there for us.

"Do they bite?" I ask.

She doesn't seem to hear me, so I ask louder, "Do they bite?"

"Does what bite, miss?"

"The horses. Do they bite? They have a great many teeth."

"Not these ones. It's in the breeding." Pride is

evident in her tone. "The house stables is some of the best around. My cousin Jasper was just made head groom, an' he—"

The sound of feet pounding down the dock interrupts her and I turn to see the boy from earlier running toward us. Something wrapped in newspaper is clutched between his fingers, and an impish grin covers his face. He cranes his neck to steal a glance behind him as one of the wrinkled fishermen gives chase, yelling that he needs to pay for what he stole. Then the fisherman calls the boy a name that I am far too familiar with. *Bastard.*

The little boy looks as if he's going to give us a wide berth but suddenly changes direction. "Here, catch!" he shrieks, balling up the newspaper and tossing it at me. A freshly caught fish is revealed.

Instinctively, I move to avoid the dirty paper. This puts me directly in the path of the old fisherman and we collide. The force is so great that he knocks me off my feet.

"Oh, no, miss!" I can hear Maddy wailing. "Mind the harbor!"

But her warning comes too late, and I hit the water with a splash. My head sinks below the surface and only then do I remember to let go of my skirt.

Trying to conserve my air, I kick as hard as I can to propel myself upward. Learning how to swim was a necessary part of life in Siam, but the heavy material of my dress, and the layers of undergarments beneath, weigh me down like an anchor around my feet. I sink farther and sputter as my lungs start to fill.

My arms flail desperately, reaching for something to grab on to, but there is nothing. Panic sets in. Every breath I take floods my mouth with dirty water. Tiny bubbles start to surround me as the air escapes my body. The edges of my vision go black, and I realize I'm not kicking anymore.

I'm going to drown at the bottom of this harbor. I'm never going to meet my father.

Suddenly, something plunges into the water beside me. I feel the force of it ricochet around my body. A hand grabs mine, and strong arms pull me toward the surface. My lungs constrict painfully when we break free of the water and I take a ragged breath, struggling to kick my legs. Struggling to be free of these murky depths.

"I have you," a voice murmurs close to my ear. "You are safe."

I can hear people shouting and then more arms are reaching for me, hauling me up onto the dock.

"Clear back, clear back!" Maddy shouts. "Give her some room!"

A man kneels beside me as I continue to gasp for air. "Maddy," he says, "loosen her stays. She cannot breathe."

His voice is gentle, and even though he's giving a command, it sounds like a request. I catch only a glimpse of dark hair and dark eyes before he pulls back and Maddy takes his place. "Just a moment, miss. I'll loosen you up."

Rolling me to one side, she deftly unties the laces at the back of my dress. The feeling is such sweet relief and I am immensely grateful to her. But then I remember my scarf. Raising trembling hands to my neck, I fear it may be lost. Another rush of relief sweeps over me when I find the linen is still there.

Maddy retightens my laces before standing again. A scowl crosses her face. "We was lucky Mr. Poe was here. The old man who tipped you in was no help at all."

She offers me her hand and I take it, slowly getting to my feet. Two men in black uniforms are beside her. One of them has removed his hat and is clutching it anxiously. Lifting my sodden skirts, I manage to awkwardly bow to them. "Thank you for rescuing me, Mr. Poe," I say to the one holding his hat.

He tips his head at me. "Forgive me, miss, but I'm Jasper."

I look to the second man, but he inclines his head as well. "Thomas, miss."

Someone moves behind me, and I turn. A young man wearing a wet gray suit takes a step forward. His cravat has come undone. Midnight-colored hair tied at the back of his neck matches dark eyes and heavy brows, though his features are refined and elegant. "Miss Annabel Lee, I presume?" His voice has a lilting sound to it. Like poetry being read aloud.

At my nod, he bows deeply. "It's an honor to make your acquaintance. I'm your father's assistant, Allan Poe."

Suddenly aware of what a picture I must present, my cheeks flame as I briefly meet his eyes and then look away. In Siam, it's considered rude to make eye contact for an extended length of time. "It's my honor to meet you, sir. I owe you a debt of gratitude for saving me."

"Think nothing of it. Your father would have my head if I let his only daughter drown." Paying no heed to the mud covering my dress, he offers his arm. "May I escort you to the carriage?"

"Of course." I take his outstretched arm and he walks me the rest of the way. When we finally reach the carriage, I stop and gaze up at it. It's a deep green color, with a leather roof to provide protection from the threatening rain, and paintings of twin golden lions upon the doors. Glass lanterns hang from the front and rear, and the interior is illuminated as well. I have never seen a carriage as fine as this.

"Up an' in," Maddy says. "Thomas will help you."

My skirt is even heavier now that it's soaked through, and I have to move carefully up the small set of steps. Maddy climbs in beside me, and Mr. Poe follows, sitting down across from us. I discreetly wipe a droplet of water from my brow and blow out a nervous breath as Mr. Poe reties his cravat.

Should I ask about Father? There is so much I wish to know.

The carriage lurches to one side when Jasper and Thomas climb aboard and then the horses start to pull us forward. I grip at my seat as the carriage rattles beneath me. It seems the stories I have been told were untrue. The streets of America are not paved with gold, but with uneven stones.

"Don't you worry none," Maddy assures me, "Jasper is a good driver."

Overhead, a sudden crack of thunder announces the arrival of the storm, and from the window, I see lightning split the sky. Trying to distract myself, I say to Maddy, "I have not yet had a chance to properly introduce myself. I am Annabel Lenore Lee."

"Madeline O'Doyle, miss. Called Maddy." Her smile is large and full of excitement. Two top teeth meet crookedly in the middle, giving her a charmingly off-kilter appearance. "I'm grand pleased I am to be yer dressing maid."

"It's lovely to meet you, Maddy."

Thunder cracks again. The rain turns terrifyingly loud overhead and I struggle not to let my panic overtake me. Ever since I was a young girl, I have had an abnormal fear of thunderstorms. And being trapped in this box, trapped in this dress, trapped in this unfamiliar corset and stays and undergarments in which I cannot breathe is too much. . . .

Just as I am about to ask Maddy to stop the carriage and let me out, Mr. Poe says, "I do not enjoy late-night storms. They remind me of the grave, rolling in with a shroud of darkness that covers the earth. Would you be so kind as to distract me, Miss Lee? Tell me how you ended up taking a bath in Philadelphia's finest waters."

I glance over at him. His gentle smile is soothing, and I feel some of my worry start to melt away. "A young boy who was being chased chose an unfortunate moment to change course. The fisherman who was pursuing him could not change his course quite as quickly. It was my misfortune to be in his path."

"And the fisherman *pushed* you in? The cad!"

"Truly, it was an accident," I say hastily. "He did not do it on purpose."

"Still, he could have stopped to help you out of the water." A muscle ticks angrily at the bottom of Mr. Poe's jaw. "If I had not been there—" He stops and then shakes his head. "Well, I guess it's fortunate I was there, wasn't it?"

He gives me another smile and I suddenly feel as if my laces are too tight again.

As we continue on, I notice Maddy putting a hand to her temple. She grimaces and closes her eyes. "Are you feeling unwell?" I ask.

She opens her eyes. "Storms make my head hurt."

I think of the times when I was plagued with

headaches. "My mother is—*was*—a practitioner of certain techniques that helped to ease head pain. I'd like to show one of them to you, if you would allow it?"

Maddy hesitates.

"I promise, it won't hurt. May I see your hand?"

Slowly, Maddy gives me her right hand. Dark crescent moons under her fingernails show a lifetime of hard work, but the bones in her fingers are small and delicate. A striking contrast to the coarseness of her palm. The third finger is swollen a bit, most likely broken and never properly healed.

I feel for the small web of flesh connecting her thumb and forefinger. Placing my thumb over the top of it while positioning my finger beneath, I press down gently. "This is where your heart and head are connected," I explain. "An invisible line pulls between the two. As I apply pressure, the pain in your head will release."

She closes her eyes again, tilting her head down slightly. Several minutes pass. Suddenly, her eyes open. "All the head pains are gone. Just gone, miss!" She looks at me with awe.

I glance over at Mr. Poe, and he nods at me. "It seems you have the gift of healing."

Feeling flustered, I look away. My heart is beating entirely too fast. "My mother was very talented. She taught me everything I know." We hit a bump, and Maddy's fingers are withdrawn from mine. She stares down at them in wonder while I look out the window.

"Passin' Rittenhouse Square," a voice from on top of the carriage says.

"Did you hear about what happened at the square?" Maddy asks Mr. Poe, leaning forward in her seat. "The kitchen staff was just talkin' this morning about how it's not safe to go out after dark with a murderer on the loose."

I draw in a sharp breath. "Murderers roam free here?"

"Although Philadelphia is a large city, you are quite safe," Mr. Poe assures me. "We do not allow our murderers to *roam free* for very long. We have an excellent police system."

"Beggin' yer pardon, miss," Maddy says. "I hope I didn't give you a fright. There's no need to worry. Yer father's house is not very near Southwest Square, an' Jasper an' Thomas walk the grounds ev'ry night."

"Southwest Square? I thought he said Rittenhouse Square?"

"They changed it to Rittenhouse last year," Mr. Poe explains. "Most of us still call it by its old name."

We ride for a little while longer, until the carriage stops and then lurches to one side again. Jasper and Thomas start to descend. "We have arrived," Mr. Poe says. "I hope you shall not be disappointed, Miss Lee."

I strain my eyes in the darkness to see. All I can make out is a large structure of pale stones, tall doors, and rows of windows gleaming like sharp teeth against the night. It looks nothing like the bamboo houses built high on stilts that I have spent the last ten years of my life in.

A sense of unease fills my stomach as I stare up at what is to be my new home. Dark and foreboding, it appears just as unwelcoming as the rest of Philadelphia.

Two

Mr. Poe steps out of the carriage first and offers to help me down. I try not to let my apprehension of the towering house in front of me show, and thank him for his kindness. Two older ladies wearing the same matching garb as Maddy are there to meet us, introducing themselves as Cook and her assistant, Johanna.

"What did you manage to do?" I overhear Cook scolding Maddy as soon as she gets a proper look at me. "Drop her in a mud puddle?"

My cheeks flame, but Mr. Poe handles the situation

gracefully. "There was a small mishap at the dock. Fortunately, Miss Lee has agreed not to hold it against us, and we can only hope she will give Philadelphia another chance to make a better first impression."

I give him a polite nod, and Cook and Johanna gather around me like protective mother hens. Their voices turn soothing.

"We'll have you cleaned up good as new, miss," Cook says. "You mark my words."

"That's right," Johanna agrees. "Nothin' some hot water an' fresh towels can't fix."

Mr. Poe bows to me. "Until we meet again. It will be sooner rather than later, I hope . . ." My heart beats like a trapped bird inside my chest as I wait for him to continue. He stares for a moment, then says softly, "Welcome to Philadelphia, Miss Lee."

The ladies erupt in a tizzy as soon as he climbs back into the carriage. They shepherd me toward the kitchen while Maddy regales them with the story of how Mr. Poe jumped into the water to save me. I am soon seated at a bench in front of a roaring fire and given a cup of tea. I take it gratefully, and marvel at the space. The kitchen alone is as big as the house that Mother and I used to share. A rough cloth is applied to my face, and then another is set upon my arm as Maddy and Johanna begin to dry me off. "Is it hopeless?" I ask. "Is my dress ruined?"

"Not yet, miss," Maddy says. "Dinner will be late this evening, so I can take you to yer room an' scrub the stains out there, if you'd like."

My spirits lift. "Where is the well? I'll help you draw some water."

Maddy stops scrubbing. "*You*, draw the water? Oh, no, miss." She shakes her head. "That's servants' work. You don't need to be doing that."

In the village where Mother and I lived, there was no such thing as "servants' work." Everyone pitched in equally, and when someone needed help, it was offered. But I don't wish to offend Maddy, so I simply bow my head in agreement.

She fills a large pot with steaming water from the fireplace kettle and then beckons me to follow her up the staircase that leads away from the kitchen.

We go to the first level and Maddy informs me that these are the servants' quarters. The hallway is dark, with only a single candle burning. I cannot see very far. Then she takes me up to the next level. "The main living quarters," she says.

I can see clearly down this long hallway because it's lined with candles. Gleaming hardwoods and beautiful, intricate fabrics grace the walls. Maddy passes several doors until she finally stops in front of one.

"Here we are. This'll be yer bedroom, miss." With a well-practiced motion, she places the pot upon her hip and takes a key from her pocket.

When the door swings open, the sight before me causes my breath to catch. Summer sunshine is captured permanently upon the golden-yellow walls, the draperies are like ripe pomegranates, and the rug is a vivid shade of burnt amber. A bed so large it could fit Mother and me a dozen times over sits in the center of the room. On the right side is a painted dressing screen, a washbasin, and an armoire, while to the left is a desk with freshly cut flowers and a matching pair of brown chairs.

Maddy puts the pot next to the fireplace, then reaches for the cords that lace up the back of my dress. I hold on to my scarf as she removes my stays and petticoat. "Isn't that wet, too, miss?" she asks.

I shake my head, feeling utterly ridiculous and more than a little exposed standing in nothing but my shift and stockings, but if she thinks me odd for keeping on the scarf, she does not say anything, and turns her attention instead to my traveling dress.

"There is a rip in the seam near the shoulder," I admit with embarrassment. "I thought I could dress myself, but I tore the fabric."

Her brow furrows as she looks for the imperfection. "No need to worry. I can stitch this right up, miss."

I stand there for another moment, unsure if I should offer to help. *Is sewing considered servants' work as well?*

"Why don't you sit a spell?" Maddy finally says. "This will be done in a dog's eye."

The bed catches my attention again, and I run a careful hand down the exquisitely embroidered quilt covering the length of it. The fabric is soft beneath my fingertips. "I don't think I've ever seen anything so beautiful," I say.

"The Grandmaster chose the furnishings for the room. The chairs an' desk were the late Grandmistress's, an' she made the quilt herself." She dips a cloth into the pot and scrubs at a spot of mud on my dress.

"Grandmaster? You mean . . . I have a *grandfather*?"

Maddy glances over at me, her face curious. "Don't you know all the family you have?"

I shake my head. "Mother spoke very little of my

father, and until I received the letter summoning me here, I thought I would never have the chance to meet him."

Maddy looks away. Plunging her hands into the water, she scrubs vigorously. She blots at several more clumps of mud and then removes the dress from the pot. "Here we are." I can tell she's forcing a cheery tone. "We'll just hang it in front of the fire to dry an' then I'll fix the tear. It'll be good as new."

I follow Maddy over to the fireplace and warm my fingers. My scarf is still damp, but I cannot remove it. Mother made me promise never to take it off in front of anyone.

Maddy hangs the dress up and then goes over to the armoire. She returns to me with a silver hairbrush in one hand and several pins in the other. "Come sit at the desk, miss," she says. "An' we'll see about fixing yer hair."

She spends an eternity brushing and pinning, and by the time she's done, I'm dangerously close to falling asleep. Then she tells me to wait while she fetches some sewing supplies. When she returns, she carries a needle and thread and my valise. "Thought you might want this, miss." She places it on the floor at my feet.

While Maddy fixes the tear in my dress, I search the valise for the gift I brought from Siam for Father. My thoughts are momentarily distracted when my fingers brush the newspaper from the dock, still within the front pocket, and I'm reminded again of the chilling headline I read.

Luckily, I'm also able to find a second gift amongst my meager belongings and it doesn't take long for Maddy to finish her task before she is dressing me again. I stow the treasures for Father and Grandfather safely away in my side pockets.

We take a different staircase downstairs, and this one leads us to a cavernous room with dark brown walls and large paintings. Without Maddy as my guide, I fear I shall never find my way back to my bedroom.

"This is the great room," she says.

Maddy returns to the kitchen and I'm startled when the adjoining doors next to me suddenly slide apart. A very tall man steps out from behind them, wearing a black suit. His hair is white, and he has the bluest eyes I've ever seen. "Ahhh, you must be Annabel," he says with a smile. "I am your grandfather. But please, call me Grand-père."

I bow deeply. As the head of this family, he deserves

my greatest respect. "Grandfa—Grand-père. I am honored to meet you."

"A bow!" His eyes light up. "What fine manners you have. It's good to see that the heathens have not ruined you."

"Just the opposite." I straighten and reach into my pocket for one of the gifts. "The people of Siam have great respect for their elders."

"Good. Good. I'm glad to hear it."

Holding out my hands, I present him with a tiny carved wooden elephant. "This is for you."

He takes it and examines it closely. A look of delight crosses his face. "Exceptional craftsmanship. Thank you, my dear. I shall treasure it." He places it carefully in his breast pocket. "Now let's call for your father so that you can meet him. Then we shall adjourn to the—"

A sound comes from the stairs, and we both turn to look at a figure standing near the top.

"Ah, there you are, son," Grand-père says. "We were just about to send for you."

The man on the stairs slowly starts to descend, leaning heavily upon the bannister. As he gets closer, I can see the reason he has need of support. His left foot is twisted—bent at an unnatural angle—and he must use his hands to lift his leg and then propel the lame foot forward with every step he takes.

I bow to him when he reaches us. "I'm honored to meet you, Father. Thank you for inviting me to your home."

He stares at me but does not say anything.

"Markus, this is your daughter," Grand-père chides. "She has traveled a very long way to be here. Surely you can say something polite."

"Polite?" Father takes another step closer. Deep lines mark his face. He looks almost as old as Grand-père. "She bowed like a man, for God's sake. Her manners are sorely lacking, and until they have been improved, I shall not encourage her."

My stomach pitches. It feels as though I'm back in the carriage again, lurching forward for the first time. "I meant no disrespect, Father. Please forgive me." My fingers bury themselves deeply in my pockets, searching for the other gift, and I offer him the most precious thing I have. "This is for you."

He glances down at it. "A rock? What am I to do with a rock?"

"It's a stone from the holy temple of Chiang Dao, blessed by the seven monks who live there. It will bring you good luck and fortune."

"Good luck saw fit to turn her face away from me many years ago. No holy rock or stone will ever change that." He glares at me, and it's only after Grand-père clears his throat and gestures at my offering that Father finally takes the stone.

I glance down at my hands. Already, I have disappointed him.

"Shall we go to dinner, then?" Grand-père says. "Cook has made a delightful roast and fresh—"

"I have a project to finish. Send something down to me," Father interrupts.

"Can't it wait for another evening, Markus? This is to be our first family dinner."

"The first of many, I'm sure." Father's tone is dismissive. "My apologies, but my work cannot wait. It's very fragile right now. I'm sure you understand."

He disappears without another word into the kitchen, and Grand-père turns to me. "Looks as if it shall be just the two of us, then. But no matter! We have a great deal of catching up to do."

I put on a smile as we proceed to the dining room. Although I'm happy for the chance to dine with Grand-père, I'm also saddened that I have already offended Father with my rough manners and poorly chosen gift.

I wonder if I shall always be such a disappointment to him.

🦋 🦋 🦋

After dinner, Maddy takes me to my bedroom and prepares the bed for the evening, turning back the linens and warming them with a plate full of heated coals. When she's done, she helps me undress. I stop her when she reaches for my scarf. "I'm rather chilly tonight. I think I'll sleep with it on if you don't mind."

She nods, and moves to add fresh logs to the fireplace while I slip between the bedcovers. Though the rain has stopped, the evening air is cool and the feeling of warm linens beneath me is a luxury I could not have imagined. Maddy comes to rearrange the blankets one last time. "All set, then, miss? If you need anything, you just push the button beside the door. It sends a loud noise right to my room. I'll hear it an' come straight-away."

Her face is so eager that I don't have the heart to tell

her I would not want to interrupt her sleep. Instead, I work up my nerve to ask her the question that's been on my mind all night. "Do you . . . do you happen to know if there's anything I might say that would please my father? What topics of conversation he finds most interesting?"

Maddy pulls away from the bed. "The other servants an' I don't have conversations with the Master. He tells us what to do an' we listen."

"Of course," I mumble, feeling foolish. "It's just that . . . I fear I have disappointed him already."

She pats my arm and her face turns reassuring. "Oh, no, miss. I'm sure you haven't done anything. Yer lovely. Absolutely lovely. The Master can be difficult to please, is all. What with his terrible sickness."

"Sickness?"

She abruptly withdraws her hand. "Never you mind now. Yer father is pleased grand to see you, I'm sure. Sweet dreams, miss. If you need me, just push the button."

I lie there long after she has gone, contemplating what she said. The house is silent and the bed is so large I feel like a ship adrift at sea. Lost amongst the bed linens. Lost amongst my thoughts.

The wind rattles fiercely against the windows, tempting me to leave the safety of my covers and peer outside to see my new surroundings. Eventually, I succumb, slipping my feet into a pair of cloth-lined bedroom slippers Maddy has left for me, and tiptoe over. There is a courtyard below.

A cloaked figure walks the perimeter, and a shiver runs through me as I remember Maddy's words in the carriage. It must be Jasper or Thomas walking the grounds. A light catches my eye on the opposite side of the courtyard, and I press closer to the glass. It's a lantern flaring to life. A figure is briefly illuminated in an open doorway, dragging a large burlap sack behind him. He limps forward, and suddenly, the lantern is extinguished.

Putting one hand up against the cold glass, I hold very still and stare down into the darkness below. *Was that Father?*

I strain my eyes for any signs of movement—*Is he still out there?*—when a loud pop comes from behind me.

My hands fly to my scarf until I realize it's only a log settling in the fireplace, and I breathe a sigh of relief. Moving away from the window, I go over to my valise and withdraw two books from the collection packed carefully inside.

One is battered and torn, with the spine badly broken in several places. This book is dearest to my heart since it once belonged to Mother. The other is my journal, and it means almost as much to me. I reach into the side pocket next and feel for the newspaper. Taking a seat on the rug in front of the fireplace, I spread the pages out before me and continue reading.

MURDER AT RITTENHOUSE SQUARE.
POLICE FIND GRISLY SCENE OF DISMEMBERMENT.

Murder most foul has been committed upon the streets of Philadelphia, whereas an unknown assailant has grievously and most purposely MURDERED a gentleman! MR. D— ELLIOT has been identified by the birthmark upon his neck and is the victim of this heinous crime. The gentleman was discovered by a house servant who found the remains at RITTENHOUSE SQUARE while traveling to the market this morning, whereas the limbs had been torn asunder from the torso and the head cleaved from his neck. POLICE urge all women and children to take heed of this atrocity and to take special cautions.

REWARD POSTED

I carefully rip the article away from the rest of the newspaper. Tucking it away into my journal, I wonder, not for the first time, if I was wrong to come to Philadelphia. Wrong to come to such a place as this. What would Mother think? Would she have approved of my traveling halfway across the world on my own? Or should I have stayed with the missionaries in Siam?

I should feel safe in my new home.

But no matter what Mr. Poe said, it is not safe to walk the streets. There is a murderer on the loose.

Three

The next morning, I wake to the sound of Maddy sweeping ashes from the fireplace. I roll over, peeking out of one eye. The draperies are pulled back and sunlight is streaming through the windows. The menace of yesterday's storm is completely gone. Light ripples across the room, and I gasp out loud when I see the floor. It's bathed in an orange glow of patterns so strange and wonderful they seem to be alive.

Maddy turns to face me with a wide smile. "Good morning, miss. It's a beautiful sight, isn't it?"

I look toward the source of the light. It's coming

from the top part of the window I'd looked out of last night. Instead of clear panes, the glass is colored. I wiggle my fingers back and forth and watch as the light bounces off of them. "It reminds me of the morning sunrise in Siam."

"It's called staining the glass. Only a skilled tradesman can do it." Maddy staggers to her feet with a bucket filled with ashes. "There are seven different ones in the house. Blue in the study, purple in the library, green an' black in the upstairs hallway, white in the Master's room, violet in the great room. Cook says they was a gift from a Prince Prospero. They're my fav'rite thing to clean." Her left cheek is streaked with soot.

I hurry out of bed and reach for the bucket. "Let me help you with that."

"No, miss," she scolds. "It isn't yer place." She brushes a hand across her face, and the soot disappears.

I glance down at the floor, hoping I have not offended her. I've never had servants before and I don't yet know what my place is. "My apologies."

"No need to worry, miss. When I finish with this, I'll be right back up to help you get dressed." She carries the bucket toward the door.

After Maddy leaves, I go to my trunk and retrieve

my robe. It still smells of *maphrao*—coconuts, as Mother used to call them—and a wave of homesickness washes over me. Even though months have passed, I still have not found myself used to the idea that she is gone. I bury my nose deeply into the worn silk. "I miss you, Mother," I whisper.

Placing the robe around my shoulders, I pad over to the windows and sit cross-legged in a patch of sunlight. It's been so long since I was last able to practice my morning meditations. On the ship from Siam, it was too noisy for me to properly focus. Even at night, when the other passengers had settled in for the evening, the sounds of the masts creaking and timbers groaning were a constant companion.

Closing my eyes, I focus on slowing my breathing and clearing my mind.

"Begging yer pardon," Maddy suddenly whispers from behind me. "What is it you are doing?"

I open my eyes and glance back at her. I did not hear her come in. "It's called meditation. It helps me to start the day with clear thoughts."

"How does it work?"

"You sit very still and clear your mind of distractions."

"How do you do that? My mind doesn't ever want to stop moving."

"Truthfully, I find that to be the hardest part," I admit. "People in Siam meditate every morning and some in the evenings, as well. I've only started practicing over the last couple of years. I'm still learning."

"What's it like there in Siam?" She moves closer, her face curious. "Is it much like Philadelphia?"

A vision of home unfolds in my mind. *Flat greenery and watery channels of a rice paddy field. Muddy rivers that connect to one another. Colorful trinkets designed for the tourists at market. Dirt roads and elephant riders. Lychee fruit and fresh mangoes. Monsoon season with its sudden torrents of rain . . .*

I describe it all to her and she listens with rapt attention.

"The elephants just walk around free as they please? Do they really have great horns on their faces?"

"Oh, yes. Their horns are called tusks and they have two of them. Elephants roam freely and are ridden like the horses are here. Only, there's no carriage, and you ride much higher up."

"I can't imagine all that rain." She shakes her head and sighs.

"It only rains that much during monsoon season.

Otherwise, the weather is clear and beautiful. Not like England. From what I can remember, it rained all the time there. Almost every day."

"You lived in England, too?"

I nod again. "My mother was born there and she took me to England when I was a young child. We stayed until I was six. Then we went with the missionaries to Siam."

I don't tell her the reasons why we left England. Or how hard life was without my father. Since Mother refused to speak of him, many labeled me a bastard child. Moving to Siam was a welcome respite from the cruel tongues in England.

"Which one felt more like home?" she asks.

"Siam. Definitely Siam," I say quickly. "We had simpler lives there, but happier ones. Mother was always smiling, and the villagers welcomed us as family."

"Then you came here. I never could've made it all on my own like you did, miss."

I glance down. When Mother and I went from England to Siam, we were stowed away on a small boat with the missionaries. They kept us safe and protected. But there was no one to protect me on the ship from Siam to Philadelphia. It was much larger, and the other passengers kept their distance. I learned quickly not to venture topside too often where I could overhear whispers about my sun-darkened skin and the scandal that I was traveling all alone.

"Do you think Philadelphia will ever feel like home to you?" she says.

"I hope so, Maddy. I truly hope so."

I get to my feet, and Maddy's eyes grow larger when she sees what I'm wearing. "Can I touch yer robe?" she whispers. Then she blushes. "Oh, forgive me, miss. I shouldn't be so bold."

I hold out my arm. "My mother gave it to me."

The tip of her finger barely brushes my sleeve before she draws back. "It's so soft. An' the color!"

"I would have packed another to give to you had I known you would like it so much," I say regretfully.

"Oh, no, miss. I could never take such a gift!" She glances down at the pocket watch attached to her uniform, and panic briefly crosses her face. "Listen to me going on an' on. I've near talked yer ear off. Best hurry now. We have to see to yer toilet an' get you properly dressed. We mustn't be late fer breakfast."

❀ ❀ ❀

Grand-père is waiting at the bottom of the stairs when Maddy and I finally make our way down, but Father is nowhere to be seen. I have to keep reminding myself not to follow Maddy into the kitchen and offer to help her with breakfast. That is not my place anymore.

"Good morning," Grand-père says. "Did you sleep well?"

How do I tell him that visions of being murdered in my bed caused me to toss and turn most of the night? "My bedroom is lovely," I finally reply, "but I think my new sleeping arrangements will take some getting used to. Did you sleep well?"

"I slept excellently. Thank you for asking."

He leads me to the dining room, where a sideboard has been set up with every breakfast dish imaginable. The sight before me is almost too much to take in. Breakfast in Siam consisted of hot black tea, rice porridge, and *pa-tong-goh*, which was my favorite—bits of dough cooked in lard, with crispy outsides and soft, sweet insides. In front of me now is surely enough food to feed the entire village.

Grand-père moves to a small stack of gleaming china at the far end of the sideboard and picks up an empty plate. He starts to fill it with food, so I move to follow his example. Then I stop and study what's on a platter next to some poached eggs. "Grand-père, what are these dark brown things here?"

"Those are kippers, my dear. Fish."

The kippers don't look like any fish I've ever seen before. But the thought of fresh fish reminds me of home, so I fill my plate with two of them and add a boiled egg. When I sit down at the table, I cut off a piece of the kipper and bite into it. It's dry and leathery. I force myself to swallow. The taste is indescribably gruesome.

Reaching for my water goblet, I take several sips to try and wash the flavor away, when Father finally enters the room. He seems to be having an easier time walking this morning, but it's still an obvious struggle. His coat is rumpled and his bow tie hangs in loose ends around his neck. A newspaper is tucked under one arm and he thumps it down across the table.

"Where is the coffee?" he says crossly. "Why can it never be waiting for me as I have requested? Is that not a simple task?"

I open my mouth to ask him if he's slept well but then think better of it. He has not acknowledged me yet. "Good morning, Father," I say instead.

He waves a hand in my direction and closes his eyes, slumping in his chair. "Cook!" he yells. "Maggie! For the love of God, someone bring me some coffee!"

It's Maddy, not Maggie. If you cannot get her *name right, do you even know mine?*

Turning my attention back to the kippers, I punish myself for my wayward thoughts and force another piece into my mouth. It's even worse the second time. I reach for my water again and drain it dry.

Right on cue, Maddy enters the room, bearing a tray filled with a water pitcher and a silver pot. I give her a smile when she stops to fill my glass first. Father's cup is next, and her fingers tremble as she fills it with coffee. But the dark liquid seems to instantly put him in a better mood. He reaches for it before she's even done pouring and manages a gruff "Thank you."

Maddy curtsies and goes to pull the pot away, when a loud scream suddenly comes from the kitchen. She narrowly misses knocking over the water pitcher as we all look up. After another cry, I quickly stand. I must find out what is wrong.

Hurrying into the kitchen, I discover Cook and Johanna bent over the sink. Johanna has a rag held tightly to her finger. A red stain blossoms on the fabric and she grows paler by the second.

"What happened?" I ask.

"Johanna cut herself peeling potatoes," Cook says frantically. "It's bad."

I put a hand on Johanna's back. "May I look?"

She nods.

Pulling back the blood-stained cloth, I see a jagged cut bisecting the middle section of her forefinger. The skin has split and peeled away from the bone. "I need a needle dipped into some boiling water and some thread," I tell Cook. "*Quickly.*"

Cook reaches into her apron and pulls out some thread, then hurries to a nearby cabinet. Removing a needle from a drawer, she brings me the thread and puts the needle into a pot on the stove. "Water for the potatoes," she explains.

I hold the rag tightly to Johanna's finger as I wait for Cook to fish the needle back out. She carries it over to me in a large spoon. The needle is hot, but I know I must work quickly. "This may hurt a bit," I tell Johanna, "but it's necessary. The cut has to be closed so that it can heal."

She bites her lip and closes her eyes as I work hastily to sew the skin back together. I've watched Mother perform this task many times, and I used to practice my sutures on a spare piece of cloth whenever she would let me. By the time I have finished, Johanna's face is dotted with sweat and my fingers are speckled with blood, but no sound has escaped her lips.

"Be sure to check it every day for signs of pus or discoloration." I tie off the thread in a knot. "If you see either of those things, let me know immediately. And avoid using it, if you can."

"I will try, miss." She nods her head. "Thank you for helping me."

"You're very welcome." I go to the sink to wash my hands. "You did well, Johanna. You kept calm and were very brave during the sutures."

She offers me a proud smile. "My sister cut her foot when we was younger, an' I stayed with her the whole time it was bleeding. I just told myself to keep steady, just like I told her."

"Keeping calm is the most important part of . . ." My voice dies off when I turn and see Father and Grand-père standing right behind me. I lower my eyes and stare down at the floor.

It's Grand-père who speaks next. "Well, that was quite an event. Who would have thought we would have need of a doctor's services this morning?" He pauses, and when I look up again, he's giving Father a sharp look. "Thank goodness you were able to offer assistance when it was needed, Annabel," he continues. "We are most grateful to you."

I don't know how to respond. Should I thank him for thanking me?

"Now that the excitement has passed, let us return to the dining room to finish our breakfast."

He and Father both turn back toward the table, and I follow silently behind. We are seated, but the room remains silent, and all I can think is that I have done something wrong again. *Was it not my place to help the servants?*

I look up when I feel someone's gaze. Father is staring at me.

"Where did you learn to do that?" he asks.

"M-mother taught me." My voice catches. "One of the missionaries we lived with was a doctor. Mother worked for him, and I was her helper."

"And this work, it involved sewing up body parts?"

"That's enough, Markus," Grand-père says sharply. "This is not suitable breakfast conversation. Especially now that we have a young lady in the house."

Perhaps now is the time to let Father know of my interests in medicine. "Such conversation does not bother me," I volunteer. "I hoped that by coming to Philadelphia, I might have the chance to further my medical knowledge. According to a book I have, written by one of the first female surgeons, Dr. Elizabeth Blackwell, the human body is—"

"A female cannot practice medicine." Father cuts me off. "It's against the law. I don't know what book you claim to have been reading or where you came upon it, but it was most certainly written by a charlatan."

"It came from a bookshop in England. Mother got it for my birthday last year, and I've been studying it because I wish to become a surgeon as well."

"Women practicing medicine is unseemly." Father's words are sharp, like tiny bits of glass, and revulsion is written clearly all over his face.

Tears gather behind my eyes. *He is disgusted with me. Disgusted by a daughter who wishes to practice medicine.*

"I think the pursuit of medicine is a noble goal," Grand-père offers. "Who knows what the coming years will bring? We may find more and more women in the medical field."

"Women do not now, nor will they ever, have a place practicing medicine. Can you imagine? A *woman* doctor?" Father's revulsion turns to anger. "No daughter of mine is going to study medicine. I forbid it." He attempts to rise from the table and it is a labored effort. "Now I will bid you a good day," he finally says, standing again. "When my assistant arrives, pray do tell him to come see me directly."

Grand-père stays silent and I cut up the remaining bits of kipper as Father exits the room. I don't think I can bring myself to eat any more of it, but at least the process keeps my fingers occupied. Unfortunately, I cannot say the same for my thoughts. Although I will not let Father deter me from my dreams, it's clear I have disappointed him.

Yet again.

Four

As soon as breakfast is over, Maddy escorts me to another grand room. This one has fine china on display and several seating areas. She tells me it's the drawing room and says I am to wait. I have no idea why I've been brought here, until I'm introduced to a woman with a severe bun and a stiff brown dress. Her face is unmovable. Much like her dress.

"Good morning," she says briskly. "I am Mrs. Tusk. Former headmistress of Menard's School for Girls, and I am to be your tutor. We shall begin our lessons immediately."

I bow to her and then immediately remember Father's annoyance with the gesture. "Forgive me," I say. "Where I'm from, it's appropriate to bow when introductions are being made. Though my father does not seem to approve."

Mrs. Tusk sniffs once and straightens the edges of her collar. "He is correct. Bowing is not ladylike. It implies a lack of proper upbringing. A curtsy or a hand clasp is the only respectable way to greet someone when you are being introduced."

She looks at me expectantly and then gestures to a nearby chair, waiting to speak until I have taken my seat. "I would normally start with an introduction to elocution and etiquette, but since I—and all of Philadelphia, I can assure you—have been informed of the *incident* that occurred yesterday, such behavior necessitates that we immediately attempt to repair the damage done. Therefore, we shall begin with the importance of one's reputation."

My voice is barely a whisper as I say, "What incident has occurred?"

"Why, the *incident*"—she sniffs again as she pronounces the word—"that resulted in your appearing in a *scandalous* state in front of a gentleman. I heard your clothing was entirely *soaked through*. You must think of what people will say!"

I bow my head in shame. Father cannot be pleased by the fact that I have caused a scandal before I even arrived.

"Reputation is your most prized possession." she says. Her shoulders straighten, and she lifts her chin. "You must zealously guard it at all times. A proper lady does not walk alone with a gentleman, and she does not speak to a gentleman unless accompanied by a chaperone. Once in the correct setting, polite company will mean polite small talk. Acceptable topics are matters such as the weather or gardening. You must take care not to speak too much, or speak too intensely. A lady never gives a gentleman the wrong impression."

I try to remember all that she's saying.

"One must never, ever be caught in a state of undress or dishevelment in front of a gentleman." Mrs. Tusk straightens her cuffs and gives me a disdainful look. "It is simply not done in polite society."

I wonder what I will have to do to repair my reputation now that I have sullied it by committing every grievous sin on her list of admonishments. Albeit unknowingly.

Mrs. Tusk then crosses back and forth in front of me. "A most important part of a lady's reputation is decorum. The way you hold yourself. The way you walk." She turns slowly and gestures down at the floor. "Feet slightly apart, never spread more than your foot's length, with arms at your sides. Your head should be held erect, and you should maintain a pleasant demeanor." Her lips part into a semblance of a smile, and she walks the floor again, nodding at imaginary people. "Now it's time for you to try."

I get to my feet and try to imitate her stance, but I'm "too stiff." "Too loose." "Too hasty." When I have walked the floor again and again and it feels that I'm finally beginning to make some progress, Mrs. Tusk merely sniffs and turns away. "Practice makes perfect. It shall certainly take time to prove this point with someone of your . . . limited background."

Dropping my arms, I feel an ache in my shoulders. If I am ever going to be as stiff and proper as she is, this part of my education is going to require a vast amount of practice.

Moments later, a knock comes on the door and Maddy enters the room. "Beggin' yer pardon, but it's time fer Miss Annabel's wardrobe fitting."

Suddenly nervous, I fidget with my scarf. I thought that perhaps I would help Maddy sew another dress or two that I could wear. I had no idea I was to be given an entirely new wardrobe.

"We shall continue upon your return," Mrs. Tusk says. "You are dismissed."

I stand and offer her a curtsy, and she gives me a brief nod. Then I follow Maddy out of the room. "Is it going to be terrible?" I whisper. "I have no idea what to expect."

"Yer going to be poked an' prodded," she whispers back. "But Madame LaFleur is the best seamstress in all of Philadelphia. Don't you worry."

She leads me to another sitting room, where piles of silk and lace already cover the floor, and two women are flitting around like busy bees. They introduce themselves as Madame LaFleur and her assistant, Jacqueline. I glance over at Maddy. *How will I be able to keep my scarf on during the fitting?*

"Go on, miss," she says with a wink. "I already told them that yer not used to the cool air in Philadelphia yet, comin' from Siam an' all, so you have to keep yer scarf on so you don't catch cold. They'll not be asking you to take it off."

I silently vow to repay her act of kindness. "Thank you, Maddy."

She gives me a curtsy, and then leaves me to face the seamstresses on my own. They direct me toward a dressing screen set up in the middle of the room and tell me to wait behind it. Moments later, Madame's assistant joins me and begins to strip me free of my dress. Bolts of deep blue and dark red silks are held up beside my face, but each one is quickly discarded when Madame comes behind the screen.

"No, no." Madame shakes her head. "These colors are not right for her. You can tell from where she has been covered beneath her clothes, Jacqueline. See? Her darkened skin, it is from the sun, *oui*? Yes?"

I nod, and she nods as well.

"Her natural coloring is fair, with medium brown hair and dark eyes. We must stay away from the dramatic."

Jacqueline puts a measuring string against my body, marking her place with one finger. Then she brings over a thin piece of muslin and a pair of scissors. Quickly cutting away two sides of it and bidding me to hold out my arms, she pins the muslin around my shoulders.

Madame makes several notes on a small slip of

paper, then mutters, "We shall need three walking dresses, five morning dresses, a cloak, some gloves . . ." She glances down at me. "Your hands?"

I offer them to her, and a look of horror crosses her face.

"*Mon dieu!* So rough, so worn. And the spots! We shall need the gloves right away. Jacqueline! Bring the extra pair. I just hope they fit."

Shame washes over me. My job as Mother's assistant made it impractical to have impeccably kept hands. Most days, we would find ourselves helping with daily tasks such as hauling water or washing soiled linens. I did not realize that here in Philadelphia even my hands would cause offense.

They pin me and mark me for what feels like several more hours until finally Jacqueline helps me dress again. She leaves me to fasten my own stockings, but she doesn't go far. I can hear her speaking softly just beyond the edge of the screen.

"Hurry," Madame admonishes. "We need to pack the fabric up quickly."

"I'm sorry, Madame. I—"

"No matter. Just be sure that nothing is left behind."

"Have we been here too long?" Jacqueline asks.

"Far too long. Even though we came in via the servants' entrance there is still risk that someone will see us leaving this house. I may have been willing to offer my services for a pretty penny, but that does not mean I am willing to compromise my reputation. Quality breeds quality, you know. Heaven forbid word get out that I have been associating with the master of this house. No matter how much extra he pays."

She says *master* like it's a foul word, and Jacqueline makes a sound of agreement. I carefully readjust my scarf around my neck, patting it into place as I contemplate their words. Why would she wish to not be associated with Father?

Once I'm fully dressed again, Madame tells me my new wardrobe will be ready in one week and then takes her leave. I return to Mrs. Tusk and we are about to resume our lessons once more, when Grandpère joins us.

"Excuse me for the interruption, but I was hoping that I might be able to steal my granddaughter away," he says. "You are more than welcome to take tea in the dining room during this hiatus, Mrs. Tusk."

Mrs. Tusk reluctantly agrees. Then she asks, "Will I have a chance to speak with the master of the house this afternoon? We have some, ah, unfinished business."

"His customary teatime is three o'clock. I'll inquire if he can see you then."

Though it is evident she has a desire to be more insistent, Mrs. Tusk only frowns slightly before turning away from us. Grand-père offers me his arm, and we walk toward the great room.

"How are things progressing with your lessons?"

I glance down. "Well, I suppose."

He notices the hesitation in my voice.

"It certainly doesn't sound as though things are going well. This is your home now, Annabel, and I want you to feel comfortable here. Did breakfast with your father this morning upset you?"

"I'm afraid *I* am the one who has upset him, Grand-père. I wish to study medicine, and he thinks it unseemly. I am nothing more than a disappointment."

Grand-père sighs heavily. "Your father is disappointed with himself. With his . . . limitations. He has an illness that weakens his muscles. He is mostly affected in his legs, as you have seen, and he deals with pain every day of his life. It does not often allow for a cheerful disposition."

"What kind of illness does he have?"

"A severe form of typhus." Grand-père's voice catches. "I took him on a trip to France many years ago, and he caught the disease there. It is incurable."

"I'm sorry to hear that, Grand-père."

"I think it's difficult for your father to remember his life before he had this affliction. The memories can sometimes drive him to the edge of madness. You must understand. I do not wish to make excuses for him, but now, it's like living with a different person."

We continue walking as Grand-père reminisces about how things were like before Father's illness struck, and I find myself caught up in his stories. It seemed like Father was so happy before the symptoms of the disease ravaged his body. So full of life.

Perhaps if I can find a way to ease some of Father's pain with one of Mother's poultices, some of that joy will return again. Perhaps then, he will come to appreciate my interests in medicine.

Five

When my lessons with Mrs. Tusk have concluded for the day, I return to my bedroom. The few medical books that I brought with me are still within my valise, and I quickly find the one I'm looking for. Paging through my worn copy of William Cowper's *The Anatomy of Humane Bodies*, I come to the topic of typhus.

> *The disease of Typhus; more commonly*
> *known as jail fever; is capable of afflicting*
> *the mind as well as the body. Head pain,*

delirium, and stupor are noted symptoms as well as nausea, arm and leg pain, body fever, and red sores. These sores can lead to rotting flesh and gangrenous limbs. Believed to be caused by rats, the best prevention is to keep one's home and property as free from vermin as possible. Once the disease has spread, there is no known cure.

But something about the entry bothers me, and I reread the information over and over, trying to decipher what has disturbed my thoughts. A knock on the door interrupts my concentration.

Maddy enters, bearing a silver tray with a teacup and a small white bowl. The bowl is filled with shiny red things. "Cook sent these along with some tea, miss. Picked fresh from the tree outside."

Remembering the distasteful kippers from this morning, I lift the bowl carefully to my nose. The red things smell sweet. "What are they?"

"Cherries. Try one. You'll like them."

Placing the cherry on my tongue, I almost swallow it whole before she laughs and stops me. "Not the green stem, miss. An' mind the pits inside."

I remove the stem and bite down, pulling out the pit. A bit of juice splashes onto my wrist and I hastily wipe it away as a sharp burst of tart sweetness fills my mouth. Maddy is right—I *do* like them. I eat several more, and glance out the window. Remembering the lantern that flared ever so briefly last night, I look farther down into the courtyard. There are bushes cut into strange shapes, and I can see the door where the figure with the burlap sack had been standing.

"Would it be possible for us to take a walk around the courtyard?" I say impulsively. "It's still daylight, and I have not yet explored the grounds."

"I'm not needed in the kitchen until dinnertime," Maddy admits. "An' since it's not dark yet, we should be just fine."

Her words give me pause. "Is it not safe to walk in the courtyard at night? I thought that's why Father has Jasper and Thomas walking the perimeter?"

"Us servants don't go out at night is all I meant, miss," she says. But she will not meet my eyes. Then just as suddenly, her grin returns. "Cook made her famous cherry jam this afternoon. It's the best thing you ever tasted. An' I know where she keeps it. I can gather some biscuits an' put it all in a basket to take with us." Her smile turns bashful. "That is, if you would want to, miss."

"A picnic! That sounds lovely, Maddy."

Leaving my medical book behind, I follow her down to the kitchen. Something sugary-sweet fills the air, and I stop and inhale deeply as Maddy gathers biscuits and cherry jam from the larder. The scent reminds me of *pa-tong-goh*. Another wave of homesickness washes over me.

"It's taffy, miss," Cook says, noticing I've stopped in my tracks. Both of her hands are plunged deep into a bowl on the table.

"What's taffy?"

"A bit a molasses, some butter, an' sugar. You heat it all up, then roll it out flat. As it cools, you grease yer hands, then pull it apart with ev'rything you've got. They're the Master's fav'rite." With a nod of her head, she gestures to a tray filled with golden-brown lumps. "Go ahead an' take a couple. They're ready."

I reach for the taffies, but Maddy waves something at me. "Waxed paper. Use this so they don't stick together."

I take the paper and wrap each one up tightly, then thank Cook and hand them over to Maddy. She puts them into the basket and leads me to a door that takes us outside. We step into a walled courtyard where the grass is lush and neatly manicured. The bushes are cut into the shapes of animals, and in the middle of the courtyard is a pond filled with orange-and-white fish.

I follow Maddy to a bench beside the pond as she points out different animals along the way. There are lions, horses, and something with small horns called a stag. We lay out the biscuits and jam between us, and our conversation slows while we eat. She seems as content to indulge in her thoughts as I am in mine. It's only when I hear a soft snore coming from her that I realize she isn't merely lost in her thoughts. Her head has drifted to one side, and her eyes are closed. She's sleeping.

Carefully placing the cloth that held the biscuits and jam back into the basket, I get to my feet. She looks so peaceful. I don't want to wake her.

We haven't eaten the taffies yet, so I put one in my pocket and leave the other two behind. Taking quiet steps over to the pond, I sit on a large rock beside it, and swirl my hand along the water's surface. I'm concentrating so hard on trying to touch one of the fish that I miss the sound of the kitchen door opening and closing. It isn't until a shadow falls over me that I realize I'm not alone.

"I hope you're not planning on taking another swim," Mr. Poe says. "I don't think that water is deep enough for you to need rescuing again."

He cuts a dashing figure in a dark brown overcoat with a leather satchel tucked under one arm, and I suddenly have to grip the stone on which I'm sitting so I won't lose my balance. I try to remember the correct way to stand, as Mrs. Tusk instructed me. *Head held high. Arms at my side. Feet slightly turned out. A gentle but not too friendly smile upon my face.*

I get to my feet and offer him my hand. "I didn't think I'd see you again so soon, Mr. Poe. What a fortunate circumstance."

He clasps my fingers briefly. "Certainly much drier circumstances than when we last met."

"That is true." Glancing away, I remember Mrs. Tusk's proper topics of conversation, but I can't seem to recall what those topics were. *What if I say the wrong thing?*

"Would you care to take a walk around the courtyard?" Mr. Poe asks, looking over at Maddy. "Since your chaperone is here, we're within the confines of propriety."

"Doesn't it matter that she's sleeping?"

He gives me a wicked smile and offers his arm. "I won't tell if you won't."

Butterflies take flight in my stomach. Desperately wishing that I had not taken off the gloves Madame LaFleur lent me, I tuck my fingers into the crook of his elbow so he won't see my rough hands. We walk to the far end of the courtyard.

"I trust you were not put off by our conversation in the carriage yesterday," he says. "Are you enjoying your new home?"

"It's quite different from Siam," I admit. "I hope it will not take very long for me to adjust." I glance up at him shyly. "And I must say, I'm very glad my father has men to walk the grounds for our protection. I saw one of them from my window last night."

"You did?" Mr. Poe looks at me curiously.

"Yes. Though I could not be certain who it was."

"Then how can you be certain it was someone walking the grounds for your protection? We *are* very close to Pennsylvania Hospital." He lowers his voice. "It might have been an escaped mental patient hoping to meet the esteemed Annabel Lee of whom we have all heard so much."

I gasp and pull away from him slightly.

"Forgive me," he says. That wicked grin returns. "I am a cad who could not resist the opportunity to tease you. You have no need to fear anything of the sort."

I cannot stop myself from returning his smile. "You gave me such a fright! Besides, I saw by the glow of a lantern . . ." My voice dies off as I recall exactly *what* it was I saw last night. Someone was dragging a burlap bag as if it were very heavy. What could have been inside?

"Saw by the glow of a lantern . . . ?" he prompts me.

"Jasper or Thomas walking the grounds," I finish. "I could not be certain *which* one it was, but I am certain it was one of them."

He studies me for a moment., the expression on his face deeply focused. Just as I have decided that he must be able to tell I'm holding something back, his face clears. "I'm sure that Philadelphia is as different from Siam as night is from day, but you haven't yet had the chance to see all that Philadelphia has to offer. Beautiful gardens, historic buildings, notable citizens. When I have a free moment from my work, I shall arrange a tour."

"That would be lovely. Thank you." Though I'm

intrigued by the mention of his work, I try to make it appear as if my interest is in nothing more than the flowers we are passing. "Do you work with my father every day?"

"Every day. Every night. At times, it almost feels as if I live here."

My heart speeds up at the thought of running into Mr. Poe in the halls. "Are you helping him with his most recent project?"

He nods. "I am."

"What kind of work does my father do?"

"He has . . . scientific interests. It's all very complicated and quite boring, I assure you."

The sun shifts overhead and disappears behind a cloud. I shiver involuntarily. Mr. Poe notices and immediately withdraws his arm from mine. "You're cold." He takes off his overcoat. "Allow me?"

Waiting for my nod, he places the coat around my shoulders. His hands pause and our eyes meet. My cheeks grow warm and I turn my head, purposefully looking at the gardens. "The roses are quite beautiful. I wonder what kind they are."

He pulls back from me and offers his arm once again. "I'm afraid I don't know. I don't spend much time in the gardens. All of my free time is spent on my—"

He stops and looks away.

I wait for him to continue. When he does not, I say, "Surely you cannot mention something so intriguing, and then not finish telling me what it is you are working on?"

"My apologies." He dips his head. "It's not something I speak of very often. What little free time I have is spent working on stories and attending poetry readings. I am a writer."

"You are?" I turn to look at him more fully. It's no wonder his voice is so delightful. He has experience reading aloud, as I thought. "Have you been published?"

"Not yet. Though I'm working on a book of poetry. It is to be called *Tamerlane and Other Poems*."

"What a beautiful title. Does it have special meaning? I've never heard of a Tamerlane."

"It's the name of the hero in one of my poems. A warrior who lost his greatest love."

"There's nothing sadder than a tragedy. I, too, like to write. But only in my journal. I wouldn't have the courage to consider writing for publication. You're very brave, Mr. Poe. I do hope one day I shall have the chance to read your book."

He stares deeply at me. I did not notice before that his left eyebrow has a slight scar above it. "I hope you shall, too."

A sudden clattering disrupts us, and we both turn to see Maddy sitting up. She's knocked over the picnic basket in her sleep, and the noise must have awoken her. She scans the courtyard, alarmed, until she catches sight of me, then hurries to join us. "There you are, miss. I thought you were—"

She's suddenly cut off by the sound of the kitchen door opening. Jasper and a large, rough-looking man step out from behind it.

"This here's the courtyard," Jasper says to the man. "We walk the perimeter at ten o'clock in the evenings."

I glance over at Maddy. "Who is that?" I whisper.

"Never seen him before." Her voice is as quiet as mine. "There was talk this morning that the Grandmaster might bring in another person to walk the grounds on account of the most recent murder. But I don't know him."

Jasper glances our way and then doffs his hat. "Miss," he calls out. "Master Allan." They move closer, and Mr. Poe takes a step forward, placing himself in front of Maddy and me.

When they come to a stop, Jasper gives us a brief bow, but the man beside him does not. His clothes are worn and dirty, obviously not well kept, and his eyes dart back and forth nervously. "This is Brahm," Jasper says. "He's been hired to walk the grounds."

Brahm shifts his weight from foot to foot, seeming only to grow more nervous by the second. He mumbles something that I can't quite catch.

After a brief moment of silence, Mr. Poe says, "We should return to the house. The air is growing cooler as night approaches. I would not want either of the ladies to catch cold."

Jasper nods, replacing his hat as we turn away, and Maddy walks by my side. We stop by the bench to pick up our picnic basket. "I don't like him," she mutters, casting a glance back at Jasper and Brahm. "Something doesn't sit right."

I feel bad for the new night watchman. Perhaps he is merely as unaccustomed to his unfamiliar surroundings as I am. "If Grand-père hired him, then he must be a trustworthy person. Is that not so?"

She only shakes her head, and casts him another grim look.

We return to the kitchen, and just as we're about to step inside, I realize I'm still wearing Mr. Poe's coat. I remove it and give it back to him. "Thank you for the lovely walk and the use of your jacket. It was very kind of you."

"It seems it is my duty to save you from the elements, Miss Lee. First the water, and now the wind."

I blush at his words. Remembering the taffy in my pocket, I offer it to him along with my hand in goodbye. "For you, Mr. Poe," I whisper.

"Please, call me Allan." Bending low, he kisses my hand and takes the taffy. "Until next time."

I can barely find my voice. No one has ever kissed my hand before. I stare up at him, suddenly glad that I have come to this strange, new place.

"Until next time . . . Allan."

Six

I'm distracted with thoughts of Allan during dinner that evening, but Father and Grand-père don't seem to notice. Father is alarmingly pale and listless. He refuses to eat anything, and his eyes keep closing. Just before the third course, he stands and asks Thomas to help him up the stairs. They stumble several times on their way out of the room.

"Is he going to be all right?" I ask Grand-père, casting an anxious look after them. Father's illness seems to be taking a heavy toll on him this evening.

"Some brandy and bed rest will do wonders. He'll be fine in the morning."

We sit at the table for four more courses, though I don't eat very much. Dinner in Siam was usually freshly caught fish and jasmine rice. I'm not accustomed to the rich sauces and heavy meats that are served here. I apologize to Maddy for leaving so much behind when she comes to take my plate away each time, but she assures me that it will not go to waste.

When dinner is finished, I bid Grand-père good night and retire to my room. Maddy helps me undress, but I cannot sleep. Wrapping a dressing gown around my shoulders, I pad over to the window to see if anyone is in the courtyard. But clouds fill the sky, casting their shadows on everything below, making it impossible to see anything. My stomach starts to ache, so I decide to go down to the kitchen to see if I can find some biscuits to relieve it.

Retrieving Mother's battered book from beneath my pillow, I tuck it safely into my pocket. With it next to me, I do not feel so alone. I take the lamp from the bedside table, and then find my way down the long hallway that leads to the main staircase. The house is quiet. Everyone else must be asleep.

When I finally reach the kitchen, the yeasty smell of dough for tomorrow's breakfast fills the room. I find a tin of biscuits in the larder, and my stomach stops aching as soon as I've eaten one. I put another in my pocket to take with me and go back to the staircase, lifting the lamp high to study the portraits with names engraved at the bottom of each frame that line the stairs. It appears to be a family history—*my* family history.

Father's portrait is the most striking. He looks so young and happy. His face smooth and unlined, not yet furrowed by the effects of his illness.

"A fine likeness, I assure you. Although it does not bear much resemblance now."

A voice comes from behind me and I gasp, almost dropping the lamp.

"I'm sorry, my dear. I did not mean to frighten you." Grand-père is still dressed for dinner, though his cravat has been loosened and he wears slippers. "I saw your light from my study. I take it you couldn't sleep, either?"

"I . . . I was feeling ill and thought some biscuits might settle my stomach."

"Don't tell Cook, but goose liver always upsets my

digestion as well." He gives me a kind smile. "Come with me. I have something that might help."

I follow him into his study. A large desk sits in the middle of the room, with a framed piece of parchment displayed prominently on the wall behind it. As I move closer, I see the words *The Unanimous Declaration of the thirteen united States of America* written across the top of the paper. On either side of the frame, long plumed pens are hung. Grand-père gestures for me to take a seat on a couch opposite the desk, and I do so.

"Is that something you have written, Grand-père?" I ask, nodding toward the frame.

He casts a glance at the wall. "That? Oh, no, my dear. That is hanging there because it is a piece of our history. Composed by Thomas Jefferson and adopted not far from here at Independence Hall. This document was how our great nation of America was born."

"And they gave it to you? How wonderful!"

Grand-père chuckles and opens a nearby cabinet. "Alas, it is merely a copy. But I am indeed lucky to own even that." He returns with a bottle filled with amber liquid and two empty glasses. "Just a nip now," he says, setting the bottle on the desk. He pours a small amount into a glass and hands it to me. "Here we are."

My fingers are steady as I accept the drink. The smell of it burns my nose, but I watch as he pours the second glass and sips it slowly. I imitate his gesture and a fiery path traces its way along my throat and down into my stomach, leaving behind a curiously numb sensation.

"Brandy. Good for whatever ails you." Grand-père lifts his glass high. He drains the rest of it with one swallow. I move to do the same, but he stops me. "Tut, tut, tut. You'll want to continue at a pace slower than mine. Wouldn't do to upset your stomach further."

He pours himself another glass and sits at the desk. I settle into the couch, drawing my feet up beneath me, and continue to drink slowly. The room grows warmer with every sip I take, but the warmth is soothing. As though I'm being cosseted by a soft blanket. I shift again, and the book in my pocket bumps against me. "Do you know it's the Year of the Dog?" I say.

"Is it?" Grand-père looks surprised. "And how have you come to this conclusion?"

I withdraw Mother's book from my pocket and open it carefully, trying to find the right page. My finger does not want to mark its place. It keeps moving around. "It's here." I glance down, frowning. "No, here." I'm on the correct page now, and I hold it up briefly for him to see. "This is the Chinese zodiac calendar. Based upon the *Shi Jing*, or *The Book of Songs*. It says that every year is assigned an animal, and people born during that year will share the same traits as that animal."

"Fascinating. Do go on."

I grasp the book firmly and focus on the chart in front of me. "According to the Chinese zodiac, 1826 is the Year of the Dog. People born in this year are loyal and sincere. If a dog should happen to visit your home, it's considered good luck."

"What about the year you were born? What animal do you share characteristics with?"

I have no need to look it up. I know my zodiac year by heart. "My birth date is May fifth, 1810. I was born in the Year of the Horse."

"I see!" He looks delighted. "Can you do mine?"

I place my empty glass on the floor. "When is your birth date? If you were born before February, then you might be the sign of the year ahead of you."

"You have to vow that you will not reveal to anyone

how old I truly am," he says with a smile. "The year was 1770. The date . . . May fifth."

I turn to the page that has his birth date and read his qualities aloud. "You were born in the Year of the Tiger. You are lively and engaging and incredibly brave. You are a good strategist and tactician. Horses and Dogs make good friends, but beware of Monkeys."

"And?" He waits with an amused smile upon his face.

I glance down at the page again. *May fifth* . . . "We share the same birth date!"

Grand-père nods. "A fine celebration we shall have this year. Two birthdays instead of one."

Glancing down at the book, I trace the worn spine. "It's sad that Mother will miss it. She would have been so pleased. This was the last thing she gave me before she passed."

"It was her book?"

"Yes. She carried it everywhere with her. The missionaries we lived with thought it was foolish to believe in such superstitions, but she always said that the world is a very large place and it would be foolish not to believe in a little bit of everything."

"If I may ask, how did you end up in Siam?"

"By way of England. We lived there with Mother's great-aunt Isobel until I was six years old. When Aunt Isobel passed, the house was sold and we had nowhere to go. Mother approached the local parish and begged them for a job, but they had nothing. They told us we could travel to Siam with the missionaries and work for our provisions there."

"Were it not for her letter, I'm not sure I would have found you."

"She wrote to you?"

"To your father. She told him she was gravely ill, and she asked if you could live here should anything happen to her. I answered the letter and booked passage right away for both of you to come to Philadelphia."

I frown. *That's not what Mother told me.* She said a letter had come from my father in America, requesting that I go live with him. Since she was sick, she begged me to consider the request for her sake. *Why would she tell me something so different?*

"I'm sorry, Annabel." Grand-père's voice is filled with regret. "Had I known where you were, I would have rescued you from that life. I spent years looking for you."

"Looking for me? Mother did not speak of Father

often, but I thought he was aware of our circumstances. When I was younger, I used to make up stories that he was a war hero who had gone off to battle and would one day return to sweep us away to live in a grand castle. After Mother told me about the letter, I thought the day had finally come. That he was ready to know me. All this time . . . did Father *not* know where we were?"

Grand-père glances down at his glass. "I cannot answer that."

"It was *you* who wanted me to come live here," I realize. "Not him. That's why he didn't meet me at the ship. Why he has been bothered by my very presence."

Grand-père shakes his head. "Please, my dear, do not think badly of him. He is just distracted by his illness. We are both truly happy to have you here with us."

The look in Grand-père's eyes is so sad that it makes my heart hurt. I do not wish to cause him distress. "Regardless of who answered Mother's letter, I'm happy to be here with you and Father. Thank you for everything you have done for me, Grand-père. You have shown me great kindness."

His voice is scratchy when he speaks again. "I am the

one who is thankful to have you here with us, Annabel. But we are not the only family you have. Someday soon, we shall have to take a trip to France. Our family seat is there, and we go back many generations."

I give him a smile and he raises his glass to me. His eyes still look sad, though, so I pick up my book again. "Shall we do another zodiac year? When is Father's birth date?"

"December first, 1792. I remember it as if it were yesterday. *The Farmer's Almanac* predicted twelve feet of snow, and it was right."

He continues to speak as I look up Father's birth date. December 1, 1792 is the Year of the Rat. A sinking feeling fills my stomach. My father is a rat, and I am a horse. It is no wonder he continues to be disappointed with me.

We are destined to be mortal enemies.

The clock strikes three times, and suddenly, Grandpère stops speaking. A nervous look passes over his face. He quickly drains the rest of his brandy and sets the glass down. "I did not realize how late the hour has grown. We shall have to continue this another time. Come, my dear, I'll walk you to the stairs."

The room tips to one side as I stand, but Grand-père

gives me his arm and carries the lamp. As we go back out to the great room, I see a shadow moving toward the dining room. "What's—"

I turn my head to look, but nothing is there.

Grand-père glances at me. "Is something the matter?"

I stare into the darkness. "I thought I saw something. My eyes must be playing tricks on me."

"Yes, yes. That must be it." He urges me toward the staircase, then hands me the lamp. "Here you are now. Up to bed with you. I don't want to be the cause of your losing any more sleep."

"Time spent with you is surely worth any amount of lost sleep, Grand-père. Thank you for sitting with me."

"The pleasure was mine, my dear. Though perhaps it would be best for you to take some biscuits at breakfast in the morning to keep in your room in case you feel ill again. You should not be down here so late at night. The house can get . . . rather chilly."

"Of course, Grand-père."

He bids me good night and returns to his study. I take several steps up the stairs, then come to a stop. *I should go apologize to him. Clearly, I should not have been wandering so late at night on my own.*

But when I turn around, Grand-père is standing outside the study doors with his back to me. He glances over at the dining room. And nods to the shadow that I thought I had only imagined.

Seven

With my head full of strange thoughts, I walk slowly up the stairs. *What's going on in this house? Why are there mysterious shadows at night, and clandestine deliveries in the courtyard? What made Grand-père so nervous and why did Madame LaFleur say she did not want to be associated with Father?*

It isn't until I've settled beneath the covers once again that I realize I've forgotten Mother's book downstairs.

Leaving the lamp behind, I instead take one of the candles from the hallway to light my path downstairs.

When I reach Grand-père's study, the doors are closed but I hear a faint noise from my left. The dining room door is slightly ajar, and I approach it slowly. Placing my ear against the solid wood, I hear a thump. And then another. Then voices.

I back away. The voices are getting louder. They're right on the other side of the door now, and it sounds as if whoever is there is going to come through at any moment.

I glance over at the stairs. I don't think I'll have enough time to reach them. The door will open any moment and I will surely be seen. A long hallway to my left offers another chance at escape, and even though I have not been in that section of the house, I have no choice. I'm going to be discovered if I stay here.

I hurry down the hallway only to come to a set of double doors. Struggling to pull one open, I finally slip behind it. The room I find myself in is a library with so many books that even if I were to read one every day of the year, it would surely take me a lifetime to get through them all.

There are two levels of bookcases, and they wrap floor to ceiling all the way around the room, from one side of the door to the other. A balcony with a railing separates the upper portion from the lower portion, with the only connection between the two a spiral staircase in the far right corner. The middle of the room is filled with freestanding bookcases.

Closing the door quietly I hold up my candle to read the titles on the books closest to me. It's a section of law books, each one at least five or six inches thick. I move past them, taking note of the dust and cobwebs collecting on the shelves. No one has cleaned in here for quite some time.

As I make my way around the room, I come to an unlit fireplace with two club chairs in front of it and a small table between them. An empty glass sits on the table. *Someone has been sitting here recently.* I continue on, and find an enormous round window on the back wall that takes up almost the entire space. But it's what's next to the window that draws my attention.

Set in a small glass case, completely free of dust, are several books that look very old. Each one has a covering made from thinly stretched, tanned leather, and the bindings are hand-stitched with crude black thread that greatly resembles sutures.

I lift the glass lid to examine the books more closely. What I find inside the first one is a mystery. Crazed drawings fill the pages, along with symbols and words that I don't understand.

Returning the book to its shelf, I pick a different volume. This one is filled with words that I *do* understand. Words of science. But as I read further, my stomach turns. The text speaks of unnatural things and terrible experiments on animals. Things that no one with a conscience should ever attempt to dabble in. The implications are monstrous.

A creaking sound draws my attention away from the book, and I glance up. I'm aligned perfectly with the edges of the bookcases in the middle of the floor, and I have a clear view of the door. It's wide open.

I lift my candle. A figure stands there. The flame is shaking, and I realize my hand is shaking, too. "Who's there? Please announce yourself."

The figure does not answer but instead comes slowly toward me. His gait is strange, and a tapping sound accompanies every step he takes. For a moment, I think it might be Father. But then I realize it cannot be him. Father has never used a cane in front of me.

When he moves out of the shadows, I see it's a young man. "Allan?" I call out. "Is that you?"

He takes another step, and immediately I realize

my mistake. Brown hair hangs loose, grazing his jaw-
line, and his face is deeply lined like Father's. His jaw
is shadowed with the early stages of a beard. Although
his eyes are dark, there's something sharp and cold
about them. I wonder if I was wrong about his age.

"Who are you? Why do you roam this house at
night?"

One side of his mouth lifts into a smile. "I work
here. Who are you?"

"My name is Annabel."

"Ahhhh, yes. The inestimable Annabel Lee. I've
heard all about *you*."

He stares at me, and something in his tone makes
me touch my scarf, making sure that it's still wrapped
securely around my neck.

"I'm Edgar. Your father's assistant."

"My father's assistant is named Allan. You look
remarkably like him."

"He has two assistants, and we are cousins. Thus the
resemblance. But I'm delighted to hear that you think
I'm remarkable."

"That's not what I—"

Suddenly, Edgar notices the book in my hands.
"What strange taste in literature you have, Annabel."

I glance down and see the open page. The perverse

drawings are in full view, and I quickly close the book. "Thi—this is not mine." Realizing that it's highly improper to be alone with a man while wearing my nightclothes, I return the book to the case and pull the edges of my dressing gown more tightly around me. "If you'll excuse me, I must go. It's late."

He suddenly reaches for my arm and pulls me toward him. I'm taken aback, and don't resist. He turns my hand so that my palm is facing up. There's a faint stain on the inner part of my wrist from where the cherry juice splashed earlier, and he traces it with his thumb. His touch is warm.

"Sleep well, Annabel," he says, pressing down slightly.

The sensation makes me light-headed.

With fear, I tell myself. *You are light-headed with fear because he is accosting you.*

He abruptly lets go of my hand and turns on his heel to leave. Something falls from his pocket as he walks away, but he does not notice. I wait until the library door has closed completely behind him and then wait a moment longer to make sure he will not return, before I look to see what it is he's dropped.

It's a crumpled piece of waxed paper.

Eight

I sleep poorly that night, and my lessons with Mrs. Tusk do not go well the next morning. Though I try to concentrate on what she's saying, my mind is preoccupied. With Father not seeming to have known, or care in the slightest, where I have been for most of my life, to murderers roaming free and strange happenings in the dark, Philadelphia has not been what I expected.

Mrs. Tusk raps loudly on the arm of the chair she's standing next to when she notices my attention has wandered again. "If you are not going to concentrate on the lesson at hand, then we shall adjourn for the day. There are plenty of other students who would not be so ungrateful for my time."

I lower my eyes. "Forgive me. I had trouble sleeping last night."

She just sniffs and glances away. Picking up where she left off, she continues reading and I force myself to concentrate on every word she says. We go on for several hours, until the lunch hour is upon us. She dismisses me with a curt "Let us hope we have a more productive afternoon session."

When I've finished my meal, I hurry back so that I may apologize to Mrs. Tusk for letting my attention wander. But she's not in the dining room as I expected she would be, so I return to the sitting room to wait for her there. As soon as I hear footsteps, I rise to greet her.

I pause when I realize she's speaking with someone else outside the room.

"You were to meet with me yesterday at three o'clock, Markus. Why were you not available?" Her voice sounds angry. "We have an urgent matter to discuss. It's time for you to deliver what you've promised. Williams and I are waiting."

"I told you, I don't have time for this right now," Father says.

"When will you have the time? We had an arrangement."

"If we had an arrangement, then why is it *your* price has changed?"

"I no longer have a husband, and I must find a way to survive. It's only fair. What you've done isn't natural. Would you risk your secret getting out?"

Her voice is low, and I am conflicted. I should not be listening to their private conversation. Yet my curiosity is overwhelming. *What has Father done?*

I hear the thump of Father taking a heavy step. "You should be careful whom you threaten, Mrs. Tusk. You might regret it." He takes another step and his voice sounds farther away. "In fact, now you shall receive nothing."

"Unacceptable. It is you who will regret this. You owe me!"

At the sharp rise in her tone, I quickly return to my seat. Their conversation is clearly over and I do not wish to be discovered. Reaching for the French primer we were studying before lunch, I bury myself within the pages. Several minutes pass before Mrs. Tusk sweeps back into the sitting room. Her cheeks are flushed, and she smooths a strand of loose hair into place.

She picks up her book again and, acting as if she had not just come from a clandestine meeting with my father, says calmly, "Let us resume."

❦ ❦ ❦

In light of what I've just heard, I find it even more difficult to concentrate during my afternoon lessons, and Mrs. Tusk's attention seems equally distracted. When we are done for the day, I walk with her to the door, but all I can think of is returning to my room. There are so many things I want to write about in my journal.

Moments after she takes her leave, there is a knock at the door. I open it to find Allan standing in the vestibule. The white shirt he wears beneath a black vest contrasts starkly with his dark hair and dark eyes, giving him a wild, rakish look, and I suddenly wish I were wearing something from my new wardrobe instead of the same dress he saw me in when last we met.

"Good afternoon, Miss Lee."

My throat goes dry, and I cannot find my words. I

curtsy to him while I compose myself. "Mr. Poe, how are you?"

He reaches for my hand and holds it for just a second too long. "Better now."

Not only have my words deserted me, my thoughts have as well. He leans in with a smile. "May I come in?"

"Yes! Please forgive my lack of manners." I move out of his way and silently berate myself for losing my head.

He steps inside and then tucks my hand in the crook of his arm, pulling me beside him as if we are going for a Sunday stroll. "I've been working on something, and I must have your opinion."

I glance around uncertainly. There is no chaperone within sight. I do not wish for another "incident" to occur. Mrs. Tusk will surely mention it again if she should find out. "We are alone, Mr. Poe. It isn't proper—"

"*Allan*," he reminds me. Then he softly repeats the words that he said in the courtyard. "I won't tell if you won't."

Surely, he can hear my heart beating in my chest. It is so very loud.

I manage a brief nod, and he clears his throat. "I have

no words, alas! to tell, the loveliness of loving well! Nor would I dare attempt to trace, the breathing beauty of a face. Which ev'n to *my* impassion'd mind, leaves not its memory behind. In spring of life have you ne'er dwelt some object of delight upon, with steadfast eye, till ye have felt, the earth reel—and the vision gone? And I have held to mem'ry's eye, one object—and but one—until its very form hath pass'd me by, but left its influence with me still."

"You wrote that?"

"It's from 'Tamerlane.' I thought you might like it."

"It's beautiful, Allan. Truly beautiful. You are very talented."

He stops and turns to look at me. "I was inspired."

Suddenly flustered, I move to pull my hand away.

"Don't be afraid of me," he says quietly. Almost desperately. "Please."

"I'm not afraid. I'm . . ." *Confused. And overwhelmed. And . . .*

Anything but afraid.

A loud laugh comes from the kitchen, drifting through the open dining room doors, and then Allan is the one pulling away. But not before he brushes a quick kiss across the back of my hand. "Forgive me, I must be off. I have an errand to run for your father, and he is waiting."

I stammer a good-bye and watch as Allan strolls away from me. My whole body is warm, and I press cool palms to my burning cheecks. My stomach is churning, yet I want to go skipping through the halls. I don't know how to sort through any of these feelings. I've never experienced this sort of thing before.

※   ※   ※

I hope to catch another glimpse of Allan when he returns from his errand for Father, but I do not see him again. Father does not join us for dinner again either.

When the last course has been cleared, I join Maddy for a cup of tea with Cook and Johanna in the kitchen. As the kettle boils, I check Johanna's bandage.

"Is your finger sore?" The edges of the wound are an angry red color and I worry that infection will set in.

"A bit," Johanna admits.

"Have you been trying to rest it?"

"She has not," Cook says indignantly, gathering teacups and saucers. "I've told her over an' over, but she insists on pulling her full weight."

Johanna blushes and looks away.

"Do you have any stinging nettle in the gardens?" I ask Cook. "With that and some licorice root, I can make a salve that will draw the infection out."

Cook nods. "We have the nettle, but licorice root we're out of."

"I can get more at the market tomorrow," Maddy volunteers. She brings the tea tray over to the table and we gather around it while she pours. "It won't be any trouble."

She hands me a cup, and the warmth is soothing in my hands. "Can I go with you, Maddy? I would love to see what the market looks like here in Philadelphia."

"Of course you can, miss."

The conversation ebbs and flows as we discuss herbal remedies and poultice preparations, and it feels very much like being at home again with Mother. I take another sip of tea, and my thoughts turn to Allan again as I look down at my fingers. I don't want him to see them looking so poorly. "Maddy, do you know remedies that will soften hands?" I say suddenly. "Or something that will make spots from the sun disappear?"

"Rosewater an' lemon juice. Once in the mornin' an' once in the afternoon."

"Can I find those ingredients at the market?"

"You can. You don't need that, though, miss. Yer hands are just fine."

"But Madame LaFleur said—"

"Pshaw, what she said," Cook interrupts. "She's just full of herself. Madame High an' Mighty."

"I don't want Allan . . ." I stop, but his name has already slipped out.

Maddy grins knowingly. "I see how it is, then. It's fer Master Allan."

"Did you see he asked about my finger today?" Johanna remarks. "He saw the bandage an' asked right away."

"He's always a gentleman, that one," Cook replies.

"He's very different from his cousin, Edgar," I say. "I'm amazed they are even related."

The room instantly goes silent. Cook stares intently at her tea as Maddy and Johanna exchange glances. My cheeks start to burn when the silence wears on. *Did Edgar tell them that we were alone in the library? Has my reputation been ruined?*

"I did not know he would be in the library," I say. "Truly, I thought I was alone. Please, do not tell Mrs. Tusk."

Cook gives me a sharp look. "Did he do something to you?" she asks fiercely.

"N-no," I stutter. *They cannot know that he touched my bare wrist, can they?*

"When did you meet him in the library, miss?" Maddy asks.

"Last night. I came down for some biscuits and got turned around. I ended up in the library. He came in and introduced himself. I left as soon as I could. Forgive me if I did something wrong. I did not realize—"

"You did nothing wrong, miss," Maddy says soothingly.

"That's right." Cook nods her head. "Just stay away from him, miss. Stay away. He's a right nasty one."

"Why? What has he done?"

But the silence returns, and no one will say anything more. My frustration mounts at the overwhelming number of secrets this house seems to hold.

"Miss Annabel was telling me all about Siam," Maddy says, abruptly changing the topic of conversation. "You would never believe it."

"What a long journey it must have been, miss," Johanna replies. "Until the Grandmaster said you were coming here, I did not even know such a place existed."

Cook nods. "I didn't know the miss even existed. What a happy surprise it was to find the Master has a daughter."

I try not to let her words sting, reminded that my father was not the one who wanted me to come to Philadelphia. Instead, I join their excited chatter and tell them more about my homeland. When I find myself growing sleepy, I finally bid them good night.

But I cannot stop wondering what they wouldn't tell me about Edgar, and why they warned me to stay away from him.

Nine

I expect to have another restless night with so many questions running through my mind, but I sleep well and Maddy wakes me early the next morning so we can go to the market. I'm excited by the thought of finally having the chance to see Philadelphia.

My excitement is further encouraged when Father joins Grand-père and me for breakfast. He is dressed in a freshly pressed suit, and his mood is bright. Even his labored walking does not seem to bother him as much. Grand-père was right; bed rest has done him well.

"Good morning, Annabel," he says.

"Good morning, Father." I curtsy, and the smile he gives me makes me feel as if I have just accomplished the greatest feat in the world.

"I see your lessons with Mrs. Tusk are paying off." He whistles a cheery tune as he goes to the sideboard and begins to serve himself.

I don't understand the mercurial change in his demeanor, but I find myself wanting to please him further. "They are indeed. She is an excellent teacher."

"Yes, yes." He smiles at me again, but he is distracted.

I try to remember what Mrs. Tusk said about polite conversation. *Talk about the weather or gardening.* "The weather seems to be lovely this morning. Although I do hope the rain holds off while Maddy and I are at the market."

"Hmmmm? Are those your plans for the day? A trip to the market?"

He carries his plate to the table and I follow with my own, even though all I've taken is a small piece of toasted bread. "Cook has need of licorice root."

"Then you'll need some money." He catches sight of Maddy near the dining room door and motions her over. She offers him a deep curtsy and awaits his instruction with her eyes cast down. "Have Cook double whatever she usually spends for the week," he says, "and see that the difference is given to my daughter."

Maddy bobs her head and then disappears into the kitchen.

My heart is filled with overwhelming happiness. *I would gladly suffer through a thousand lessons with Mrs. Tusk if it continues to please him.* "Thank you, Father. I don't know what to say."

"It's my duty to provide for my daughter. Of course you should have spending money. How else are you to purchase what you need?"

I feel foolish and look down at my plate. "I . . . guess I hadn't given it very much thought." Mother and I did not have to worry about money in the village. Trades and barters were how we paid our debts.

"These are the things you must learn now that you're in Philadelphia." He lifts his fork, but pauses. "While you're at the market, be sure to stop by the butcher's shop. They have excellent mincemeat pies."

"Why don't you place an order for two pies, Annabel, and then perhaps you and your father can enjoy them during tea this afternoon?" Grand-père suggests.

I smile at him and he gives me a brief wink. "Shall I get one for you too, Grand-père? Will you join us?"

"I'm afraid mincemeat pie is something I can no longer tolerate, my dear. But I'm sure you shall enjoy it. It's a treat not to be missed."

"Yes, yes, that sounds fine." Father stands and looks down at his watch. "Three o'clock it shall be, then."

I feel as light as a feather as he leaves the dining room. My toast has grown cold, but I'm no longer hungry. For the first time since I left Siam, I'm finally being embraced by the family I came so far to see. "Father and I are going to have tea together!" I say excitedly to Grand-père.

He chuckles. "I told you he was happy to have you here. It's good to see your enthusiasm return as well."

Impulsively, I stand and give him a kiss on the cheek. "Thank you for making the suggestion." He pats the back of my hand, and then I go to the kitchen to tell Maddy of my good fortune. As soon as I enter the room, she holds something out to me.

"Here's yer money, miss."

I stare down at the banknotes in her hand. "What am I to do with it?"

"In yer armoire hangs a cloak with a pocket. It's

nothin' fancy, but it will do. Put the money in there to bring with you."

I nod and take the money. "Will you help me? So I don't spend too much? I don't want Father to think that I'm careless with what he has given me."

"Of course, miss." She grins at my excitement. "But the first step is yer cloak."

"You're right. I'll be back in a moment."

I return to my room and find a dark green cloak hanging in the armoire just as Maddy said. I carefully place the money inside the pocket, humming softly as I pull the cloak on and readjust my scarf. I can hardly believe how much Father's opinion of me has changed. Mother would be so happy.

With my thoughts on the memory of her, I cross over to the bed and pull out the zodiac book to place inside the cloak pocket. I shall carry her with me today.

When I return downstairs, Maddy is waiting by the front door. "Would you like to walk to the market?" she says. "It's not far, but I can have Jasper fetch the carriage if you prefer."

"Let's walk. I'd love some fresh air."

Maddy starts to wrinkle her nose but catches

herself. "Breathe it in by the house, miss. When we get to the market, it won't be so fresh."

I laugh and hook my arm through hers as if we are sisters. "I shall heed your advice, Maddy."

She glances down shyly and gives me another crooked grin. "Off we go, then."

We step outside and she leads me past rows of grand houses that look very much like Father's. Each one is connected with a private courtyard and a set of alleyways. Tall and majestic, they appear to touch the very sky, with carved details that rival what I'd always imagined castles to look like.

"Do you ever feel lost, Maddy? I don't think I'd ever be able to find my way back to Father's house without you. There are so many houses."

"I know these streets well. I was born near here. On the other side of town, of course. Nothing so grand as this. Just a tiny flat that I shared with my brothers an' sisters. I won't let you get lost, miss."

"You have siblings?"

She nods proudly. "I was the oldest. I have three brothers an' two sisters. They're all gone into service, just like me."

"I've always wanted to have brothers and sisters," I

say wistfully. "I'm sure that your mother is very proud of you."

"She was. But that was before—"

"Before? Have you lost your mother as well?"

"Not in the same way as you have, miss. Here we are now." She points to our left. "The market is just over there."

Maddy was right about it smelling crisp and clean by the house. Here by the marketplace, the scent of rotten fruit and spoiling meat is enough to make me choke. A river of muddy water flows down a shallow trench in front of us and I nudge her arm and then wrinkle my nose. She laughs.

A buzz of voices fills the air as we draw closer. Tents crowd in, one on top of the other, and vendors shout to be heard. I look around me to take it all in. Baskets and crates and long wooden shelves display their colorful wares, and although the people and the goods they have to sell look different from those in Siam, it reminds me very much of the market there. It reminds me of home.

Maddy steers me toward a yellow building and points to a symbol on a door. She explains that it represents an apothecary, and we go inside. The room is filled with large glass cases that hold colored bottles of all sizes. Maddy steps up to the counter and introduces me to the shopkeeper, Mr. Williams.

"Ah, yes," he says, "you are Dr. Lee's daughter?"

I blush. It still sounds so strange to hear Father's name. "I am."

"Welcome to Philadelphia, Miss Lee." He bobs his head. "May you make many wonderful memories here."

I thank him for his kindness, and Maddy asks for some licorice root and cinnamon. As he fills her order, I glance over at the shelf closest to us. I'm startled by the flesh-colored fingerlike tubes of a plant from Siam. "Excuse me," I say, "is that *khing*?"

The shopkeeper gives me a shrewd look. "You are familiar with the regional name?"

"Yes. I lived in Siam for many years."

"How interesting. It came in with our last shipment. It's called ginger here."

"How much would one piece cost?"

He looks in his ledger and then quotes me a price that is as much as Maddy is paying for the cinnamon and licorice root combined.

"Is that a fair price?" I whisper to her.

"I don't know, miss," she whispers back. "What's it used fer?"

"Fresh *kh*—ginger is used in tea, lentil dishes, soups, pastes. . . . It's very good for the digestion. Mother and I used it every day in Siam." At her nod, I say, "I shall take it, along with some rosewater and lemon juice, please." I withdraw the money Father gave to me and she shows me how much to hand over.

"We usually get a small assortment of herbs and flowers from Siam in our shipments," the shopkeeper tells me as he prepares two small packages. "You're quite welcome to come back."

"Thank you. I shall remember that for next time." Instead of curtsying, I bow to him. He returns the gesture.

On our way out of the apothecary, I ask Maddy if we can visit the butcher's shop next to order the mincemeat pies for Father. She agrees, and as we walk, we come upon a stand selling lace handkerchiefs. They are very beautiful, and the quality of workmanship is exceedingly fine. Maddy cannot tear her gaze away.

"Would you like to stop to look?" I suggest. "I don't mind."

"Oh, no, miss. Best not to stop an' want what I can't have."

The butcher's tent is not far from the handkerchief stand. His name is Mr. Higgins, and after introductions are made, I place my order for two pies. He asks about Maddy's brothers and sisters, and as soon as they are caught up in conversation, I slip away to return to the handkerchief vendor. Purchasing the handkerchief Maddy admired will be the perfect way to express my gratitude for her kindness in telling Madame LaFleur that I could not remove my scarf during my wardrobe fitting.

Choosing the one that caught Maddy's eye, I ask for her initials to be embroidered on it. The handkerchief vendor gives me a strange look when I tell her my name, but then she says that I may return tomorrow to pick it up. I hand her some money and then find my way back to the butcher's tent. He and Maddy are talking in low, urgent tones and she gestures wildly with her hands.

"There you are, miss," Maddy says. Her eyes are large and scared, and her face has grown pale. "I didn't know where you had gone. It's not safe to wander."

"Forgive me. I thought I would be gone for only a moment. Is something wrong?"

A sudden commotion comes from the tent next to us and a woman leans in to whisper to another woman, who cries out, and then covers her mouth with her hand in shock. She pulls the child beside her close to her skirts. My stomach twists into a knot. "What is it, Maddy? What's happened?"

She shakes her head. "We just heard. . . . There's been another murder."

Ten

Word of the murder passes quickly through the marketplace, and the mood turns somber. Maddy confers with the butcher again and then passes me the pies wrapped in newspaper. Our return to Father's house is not as leisurely as our original walk to the market.

I try to keep my anxious thoughts to myself as we hurry back. I don't want to frighten Maddy with my tumultuous feelings. But finally, I ask her the one thing I must know. "We shall be safe at Father's house, right? You *did* say it was not very close to Rittenhouse

Square, and since that's where the murders have been happening—"

"It didn't happen at the square, miss. It happened in the marketplace. Sometime last night."

"At the marketplace?"

She nods and fear courses through me. I glance down at the meat pies in my hand. Even the happy thought of having tea with Father cannot chase away my worry.

"They say the victim was Mr. Durham," she continues. "He used to stop by the house. He knew yer father."

I don't know what to say, so I merely nod my head. "I shall have to offer Father my condolences."

We walk the rest of the way to the house without another word, and I follow Maddy into the kitchen. Cook takes the mincemeat pies from me and puts them in the larder while I examine Johanna's wound again. It has become infected, as I feared it would. I place a warm compress on it to draw out the inflammation while I make the stinging nettle and licorice root salve. When the salve is ready, I apply a thick covering to the wound and put on a fresh dressing.

"Leave this on for three days," I instruct her. "Then

we shall change it. I'm sure everything will be just fine, but you must continue to rest your finger as much as possible. I'll look at it again once the skin has fully closed."

"I will. Thank you, miss."

She looks relieved, and I put the remainder of the salve into a pot so that it may be used again another day. Since there are still several hours until tea with Father, I retire to my room to look through *The Anatomy of Humane Bodies* and study the section on the makeup of the hand and finger. With a wound as deep as Johanna's, there could be permanent damage to the muscle. I want to be sure there is not more I should be doing. Eventually, Maddy brings me a lunch tray, but I am lost in my studies and eat very little.

When three o'clock finally draws near, I put my book aside and hurry to the looking glass propped up on the desk to see if I am presentable. My eyes are wide, and spread too far apart for my liking. A slight ring of amber circles the dark brown irises. No amount of wishing will change their color from the dull brown of a muddy river to a deep chocolate like the mahogany sheen of my desk, but I still hope for it anyway. Wisps of loose tendrils stray from the curls that Maddy set this morning, and I carefully smooth them back into place. "Hopefully, Father's good mood will prevail and he shall find no fault in you," I whisper to my reflection.

I'm pulled out of my contemplations as the hallway clock chimes three. Touching my scarf for reassurance, I straighten the edges of my cuffs and hurry downstairs. Cook is waiting outside the sitting room with a tea tray.

"May I carry that in?" I ask.

She looks taken back. "It's my job, miss."

"My hands are feeling restless and I would be ever so grateful to have something to occupy them. My nerves are getting the better of me."

"You'll do just fine, miss," she reassures me. "But if it will make you feel better . . . ?"

"It will."

With a cheerful smile, she hands me the tray, and I carry it carefully inside the room. Two wingback chairs are sitting next to a small table, and I set the tray down between them. Long minutes pass as I wait for Father. When the door finally opens, I stand to give him a curtsy. He doesn't seem to notice as he comes to take a seat beside me.

"How was your morning, Father?" I ask, trying to calm the butterflies in my stomach.

"It was rather busy."

I intend to pour us some tea, but he does not wait, filling his own cup and adding two cubes of sugar. He does not pour a cup of tea for me. After a moment of waiting for him to offer, I pour some for myself and gesture toward the tray. "I met with the butcher at the market to buy the mincemeat pies as you suggested."

He picks one up and takes a bite. Then he puts the other on a small plate and holds it out to me. "They are quite fresh."

I have no idea what a fresh mincemeat pie should taste like, but the flavor is moist and rich. A cross between a meat pie and spiced cake. Desperate to not lose his attention, I say, "The market was quite lovely. I saw so many beautiful things. Although I learned of the untimely death of one of your acquaintances; you have my condolences."

As soon as the words are out of my mouth, I can hear Mrs. Tusk's voice in my head, scolding me. *A proper young woman does not speak of such things.*

He looks up sharply. "Who told you this? What did you hear?"

"I only know that a murder occurred at the market-place last night."

"Yet you also know who the victim was. You say I knew him?"

"Yes." My voice is a whisper.

"Well? Who was it?"

"Mr. Durham."

"And how is it you were made aware that he was an acquaintance of mine?"

I shift uncomfortably in my seat and pick at the edge of my pie. I do not wish to see Maddy get in trouble for what she has said. "I heard of it in passing," I say slowly. "And then Maddy told me—"

"I see. So it was nothing more than idle gossip."

"Oh, no, Father. Truly, we were not gossiping about such things. She told me so that I might offer my condolences to you."

"I was not aware that the staff cared so much for my feelings," he says drily. "Rest assured, though, Mr. Durham was no friend of mine. He stole something very dear to me. If this was to be his comeuppance, then so be it. Perhaps he should not have been engaged in whatever activity it was that caused him to be murdered." Pulling out his pocket watch,

Father glances at it. "I need to return to my work now. I have wasted too much valuable time already."

He gets to his feet and walks out of the room without even a second glance. His tea has not been touched.

Stunned by his words, I drink the rest of my own tea in silence. No one, no matter what they have done, deserves to come to such an end. That Father can be so callous toward Mr. Durham's death chills me to my very soul.

     ❋   ❋   ❋

I dream that night of Father looming over a faceless body in the dark. I try to scream for help, but no sound escapes my lips. He mumbles about comeuppance and punishments fitting crimes as he paces back and forth, but I am trapped, cornered. I cannot scream for help. My corset laces grow tighter and tighter, choking the very air from my lungs, until my vision goes dark and I collapse. Then I hear Edgar's words in my head: "Sleep well, Annabel."

When I wake, the room is as dark as pitch. There is no moon overhead and the fire has gone out. A loud crack of thunder splits the air and shakes the house. I sit upright, clutching my scarf tightly around my neck.

Gradually, I become aware of a scratching sound coming from the window. I tilt my head toward it to listen more closely. *Something is out there.* Fumbling with the covers, I pull them back and feel my way over to the window ledge. The sound has grown more urgent. I press my face against the glass. My eyes begin to adjust to the darkness.

And then I realize I'm staring into a beady, black eye.

I scream and stumble backward. Feathers explode in a quick beating of wings, and a large black bird taps against the glass. It's a raven.

A sense of unease comes over me. In Siam, seeing a raven was considered a bad sign. A portent of secrets being kept. He cocks his head to one side and ruffles his feathers, staring at me. He taps again, and the sound echoes loudly in the quiet space. I bang on the glass to try to make him leave. "Go. *Shoo.* You are not welcome here."

But he merely turns his head to look at me once more.

"What is it?" I whisper. I stare back at him and he hops to one side. I follow his movements and see a light down below. Two figures are in the courtyard. The lantern they hold dips and wavers as they struggle with a large bag they're carrying. They move closer to the kitchen door, and the light disappears as they enter the house.

I wait for the light to reappear, but it does not.

My thoughts turn to dark things. Who would be down there? Was it Father again? Does this have anything to do with Mrs. Tusk?

I know Grand-père said not to wander, but my curiosity is too great. I light a candle and creep slowly downstairs. Holding my breath, I push the door to the kitchen open just a hair. The room appears much like the other night. Dough is rising, freshly scoured pots are drying on the worktable, and nothing has been disturbed.

But the door to the courtyard is standing open.

Hastily, I move toward it, remembering only moments before I step outside to extinguish my light. Allowing my eyes a minute to adjust to the darkness surrounding me, I find it's surprisingly easy to make out the shapes of the animal bushes, and the bench where Maddy and I had our picnic.

I crouch next to one of the lions and wait for the

lantern light to appear again. It does not take long until the pitch of low voices draws my attention to the doorway leading beyond the courtyard.

"Don't drop it now," someone says. "He pays to have 'em delivered near perfect as possible. We don't want no bruises."

I cannot place the voice.

"Aw, you try liftin' the side with the head then. It's easy for you to say. You don't have to keep thinkin' it's going to wake up an' start looking at you!"

"Quit blabbering. I didn't bring you on to talk my ear off."

I strain in the darkness to see the faces of the two men crossing the courtyard. Another large burlap sack is held between them. The lantern wavers, and I cannot see clearly.

"Don't know why he can't just get it himself," the unhappy man grumbles. "It's not hard to find a cemetery unguarded. He just doesn't want to get his hands dirty, an' leaves—"

A dull thud echoes the man's words and he grunts in pain. "Blasted bench! I walked right into it. My leg's goin' to be black as rotten horse meat tomorrow."

"That's what you get for blatherin' on. Now quit yer

complaining. One more word outta you, an' I'm keeping yer cut."

The man falls silent and they carry their delivery into the house. I wait for several long moments until they reappear at the kitchen door. Money is quickly exchanged, and then they both set off across the courtyard again. One of them limping slightly.

It isn't until I hear the courtyard door shutting and a key scraping against the lock, that I finally get to my feet. Thankfully, they did not lock the kitchen door behind them. It opens easily and I pad softly back inside.

I step into the room and take another look around. Then I hear something faint. I hold very still, and the noise comes again. It sounds like it's coming from beneath me. I move slowly toward the fireplace, closer to where the sound seems to originate, and I see a small door there. A door I've never noticed before.

A key hangs on a nail in the wall beside the mantel. I lift it free. The metal is cold and smooth, and I wrap my fingers around it, steeling myself for what I'm about to do. Carefully inserting the key into the lock, I turn it as quietly as I can. Every muscle in my body has tightened and my hand shakes when I place it upon the doorknob. I take a deep breath and try to steady my nerves, and just as I'm about to turn the knob—

Someone grabs hold of me.

I whirl around, drawing in a breath to scream. But it's only Cook. She's clutching a white shawl around her shoulders, and her hair is loose.

"That's no place fer you, miss. The whole house knows we do not go down below. The men that visit the Master at night are not the kind you'd be wise to keep company with." She tries to pull me away from the door.

"What's down there? I heard noises . . ." I do not tell her what I've witnessed in the courtyard.

She shudders. "Master's lab'tory."

"A laboratory?" I turn back to the door, but Cook pulls me away from it. "He's a scientist?"

"A doctor. Or at least he used to be."

She ushers me toward the stairs, and my thoughts are churning. "I don't understand."

"Rumor has it he lost his license because of strange experiments he did." She makes the sign of the holy cross. "Unnatural things," she whispers.

"A doctor? I can hardly believe it. Father seemed so uninterested when I looked at Johanna's finger."

"Ha!" Cook scoffs. "Don't let that act fool you. He's as int'rested as they come. Always reading those strange books, he is."

We reach my bedroom and she gently pushes me inside. As if regretting what she's already told me, she says, "Never you mind about it now. I shouldn't've said even as much as I did. Good night, miss."

"But, Cook, surely you can tell me more—"

She shakes her head. "It's not my place."

But before she goes, she glances back for a moment. "Don't go downstairs at night, Miss Annabel," she says softly. "An' please . . . Don't open that door."

Eleven

The next morning when Maddy is occupied with cleaning the stained-glass windows, I slip away from the house and make my way to the market. I know I should not be going alone, especially after news of another murder, but the need to get away from everything overwhelms me. The raven portent was right. There are many secrets being kept in this house.

As the marketplace finally comes into view, I retrace the steps Maddy and I took the day before, proceeding from the yellow apothecary shop toward the butcher's tent. I know I will pass the handkerchief stand along the way. Thankfully, I'm able to find it quickly, and Maddy's gift is ready and waiting for me. I turn to make my way back to the apothecary, then realize that none of the shops I've passed look familiar.

I turn back around, choosing a street to my left, and come face-to-face with the hanging carcass of a pig, split straight down the belly. A thick trail of flies buzzes about the creature's lifeless eyes. A second pig, this one missing its feet, hangs just beyond. Despite the gruesome sight, relief washes over me. Somehow, I've found my way to the butcher's shop.

As I move past the dead animals and come around to the front of the tent, I see that Mr. Higgins is speaking with someone. There's something familiar about the customer's silhouette, and when he swings a cane, I see it's Edgar. He passes several banknotes over, and then the butcher hands him a bag with a crimson stain in the lower corner.

With their transaction complete, Edgar turns away and I hurry after him. I know Cook told me to stay away, but surely it will be all right if I merely ask him how to find my way back to the apothecary. I follow him to the edge of the marketplace. He's taking the same path I had—the path that leads back to Father's house. He walks so quickly that I wonder why he carries a cane. He seems to have no need of it.

We are nearly to the house, when I suddenly lose sight of him. One moment he's there, and the next he seems to have vanished. Then I notice the wrought iron gate connecting Father's house to the alleyway is open. Stepping through the gate, I find myself in the courtyard.

"Fancy an afternoon walk, did we?" Edgar leans against a vine-covered wall, twisting the top of his cane. "If you wanted to walk with me, all you had to do was say so."

My cheeks grow warm. "I was turned around in the marketplace and followed you to find my way back."

"Out without a chaperone? *Scandalous.*"

He draws out the word, and my cheeks burn even more fiercely. "I was picking up a gift for a friend."

"You were doing some shopping? So was I."

My eyes shift to the bag he's holding. The red stain has grown larger. When he notices me looking, one corner of his mouth lifts in a smile. "Curious?" He holds the bag up. "If you come with me, then you shall find out what's in here. It's very scientific, I assure you."

Without waiting for my reply, he crosses the court-
yard. Everything inside me knows this is not proper.
The rules of society say I should not be alone with him.
Yet I long to see what's inside the bag.

Why must I be cursed with such curiosity?

Pushing my misgivings aside, I follow Edgar into
the kitchen. He's standing beside the small door next
to the fireplace, and I find myself coming to a sudden
stop. He sees my hesitation.

"Does your curiosity only take you this far?"

"My father would not approve of my being in his
laboratory."

"Your father's not here."

I am still so unsure.

"I won't tell if you won't."

It sounds more like a taunt than a reassurance, but
if I follow Edgar, I'll finally be able to satisfy my mad-
dening curiosity. And that's something I cannot ignore.
Though I try to talk myself out of it, I know I must see
what's behind that door.

Edgar opens the door slowly, revealing stone stairs
that disappear into darkness below. A lantern attached
to the wall holds a candle, and he takes it with him,
leading the way. As we descend, the air grows cooler.

A second door at the bottom of the stairs awaits us. Edgar pulls a set of keys from his pocket and deftly finds the right one. When he pushes the door open, the sight before me is something out of a nightmare.

My father has his own operating theater.

A giant, crudely made table stands in the middle of the room, surrounded by rough, hand-hewn wooden benches. Fresh bloodstains mar the table's surface, and an assortment of surgical instruments sit on a nearby tray. A large chandelier has been rigged overhead on a pulley system so it can be lowered to provide light.

The walls of the room are lined with shelves holding jars full of bloated white specimens, decanter bottles with peeling labels, and dirty wooden crates. The crates have burlap draped over them. A memory of last night flashes before my eyes, and I know that whatever was being delivered is inside those crates.

I take a step into the room. A sharp smell stings my nose. Something tangy, with just a hint of putrefaction below the surface. The floor is spotted with dark stains. "This is my father's laboratory?" Edgar nods, and I take another step. "I've been told he is a doctor."

"A brilliant doctor." Edgar watches my reaction. The look on his face is one of careful scrutiny. "You're not afraid of what you see here?"

"No. My mother assisted a doctor in the village where we used to live, and she let me help her with her work. I've had an interest in medicine ever since I was a young girl."

"I knew there was something different about you." He strides over to the table and places the bag on top of it. Flashing me a sly grin, he readies an empty tray. A moment later, he dumps the contents of the bag onto the tray and then holds up his prize with a flourish.

It's a heart.

It can't be human. . . .

He answers my unspoken question. "Bovine."

I draw closer to study it. The specimen is crimson and quite fresh. With the exception of its size, it looks very much like the human heart that I've seen in my anatomy book. Although the illustrations in my book pale in comparison to a real-life example. I long to touch it.

"It's beautiful, isn't it?"

Edgar speaks of the heart like Maddy spoke of the stained-glass windows, and I understand his wonder. I see the same beauty in this as I saw in the windows. "It truly is. And it has the same chambers as a human heart? A left ventricle? Right ventricle? Left and right atrium?"

Edgar picks it up, and I can almost see it beating again. "The same. I would dissect it for you, but your father needs it whole." He sounds disappointed.

When he puts the heart down again, there are bloodstains on his hands. He points to a large jar on the shelf beside me. "There's one that's already been dissected. Two calves grew as one, and their hearts fused."

I turn to look. The heart has indeed been split in half, and there are tiny white chambers tunneling through the tissue. But instead of a normal left and right ventricle, there are only two right ventricles. "It was impossible for the calf to have lived a normal life," I murmur.

"Two halves of the same whole," he says. "They cannot live together, yet cannot die apart. What do you think?"

"I think it's fascinating."

"Of course you do." He comes out from behind the table and gestures to another row of jars. "We also have two-headed pigs, another fused sheep, a three-faced dog, the bladder of a stunted horse, legs from a malformed kitten, eyeballs of a blind goat, and my favorite—the body of a rooster that was born without a head. He lived for three weeks until one of the other roosters started to peck away his—"

"My father collected these?" I interrupt. Reaching for the jar labeled SPECIMEN: MALFORMED PIG, I take it down from the shelf and peer at it closely. There are two clearly defined heads, each with their own eye sockets, yet only one snout that joins them. It truly is fascinating. I wonder what Father has learned by studying such a creature.

I go to open it, but Edgar puts up a hand.

"I wouldn't do that. The smell can be quite overwhelming."

Reluctantly, I place it back upon the shelf. I scan the rest of the jars, noting that the other specimens all seem to have some type of abnormality or malfunction. "Why doesn't Father have any healthy tissue?" I question.

Edgar tilts his head, as if measuring me. "It's not his area of . . . interest."

"What *is* his area of interest? I thought he was a doctor."

"Oh, he is. Or rather, *was*. It's all very"—he pauses

and gives me a sly smile again—"*scandalous.*"

A fly buzzes around my head, and I brush it away impatiently. "Cook told me he lost his license. Is that true?"

Edgar suddenly reaches out and swipes his thumb across my face. I pull back, but he gives me a mocking grin. "The fly returned," he offers.

"Is it true that Father lost his license?" I say again.

"Does a bird stop flying just because someone tells it not to? It cannot stop, if that's what it was meant to do."

Cannot stop . . . It's then I realize that Father must be practicing medicine illegally. That's why there are strange noises and clandestine deliveries late at night. Why I have been warned not to come down here. Practicing medicine without a license is against the law, and if word should get out, he will be sent to prison.

Edgar stares at me intently. "Ahhh, you've figured it out."

His tone makes me suddenly wary of where I am. If Edgar is my father's assistant, then surely, he has been helping him with his illegal endeavors. That means I now know not just Father's secret, but Edgar's as well. *Is Allan involved, too? Will Father be upset if Edgar's revealed what he's told me? How dangerous is it for me to know such a thing?*

I try to think of something to say that will not arouse his suspicion. I must not allow him to know my thoughts. "Thank you for sharing this with me, Edgar."

He scowls. "Why are you thanking me?"

"It was very kind of you to bring me down here. Thank you for showing me Father's laboratory."

"I did not do it to be *kind*. I did it because I thought you would be scared." He watches me carefully. "But I suppose it *is* in your blood. You were never going to be scared by any of this, were you? You are your father's daughter after all, Annabel Lee."

Twelve

I take my leave from Father's laboratory with the excuse that I must help Maddy with something, and quickly return upstairs. But I cannot stop thinking about Edgar's words.

What does he mean "It's in your blood?" Perhaps my fascination with the cow's heart and the specimen jars is abnormal. Are other women of medicine interested in such things?

I pace the floors of the hallway outside the dining room, strangely conflicted by my feelings. I don't wish to give up on my hopes of becoming a surgeon, yet the thought of living the rest of my life being looked at as someone who is abnormal is not something I'm sure I can bear.

I pass a small mirror hanging above a marble table, and I stop and glance into it to fix a loose tendril of hair that has come free.

But what I see horrifies me.

High on my left cheekbone is a smudge of red. The very spot where Edgar touched my face with his blood-stained fingers.

Furious, I rub at the blemish. He must have seen it. He must have known it was there. How dare he mark me like this? What if someone else saw?

My footsteps echo angrily on the floor as I decide to find something to keep my mind occupied, and head in the direction of the library. As soon as I enter, I'm drawn to the back corner again. To the case with those odd books. Are they the strange ones that Cook said Father was always reading?

Just as I'm about to select one, the sound of breaking glass comes from outside the room. I hurry to the door, and find Father there. A shattered vase lies on the floor. He's standing amongst the jagged pieces. The alcove behind him, where the vase once stood, is now empty. He must have lost his balance and knocked it off the ledge.

"Wretched thing," he mutters at the ground. Then he looks up and sees me standing there.

"I was just looking for a book to pass the time," I say. I feel as if I have to offer him an explanation as to why I'm here.

"I have need of a book as well." He glances over at the library door and then glances back to me. "Would you retrieve it for me? In the very back of the room is a small section of books in a glass case. I need the one titled *De viribus electricitatis in motu musculari commentarius*."

I know which bookcase he's speaking of. I was just there.

"Of course." Hurrying to the glass case, I find the book he's requested. I return, and hold it out to him.

But he doesn't take the book from me. Instead, he leads me into the kitchen. I'm surprised to find the room is empty. Father gestures toward the worktable, then withdraws a pocket watch. Annoyance crosses his face as he clicks the watch shut. "My assistant was supposed to be here ten minutes ago. How am I to work when he's tardy?"

I don't know where Edgar has gone, but I can't tell Father that I saw him just a little while ago in his laboratory.

Father looks at his watch one more time. "Worthless boy! I'm in the middle of a project, and time is of the essence. I can wait no longer." Taking a large ring of keys from his pocket, he moves toward the door beside the fireplace. He waves at the book and then at me. "You may carry that downstairs for me."

I follow quietly behind as he slowly limps down the stairs. When we reach the bottom, he takes out another set of keys and pauses. "You must not speak of anything you see down here. Do you understand? I demand my privacy."

"I understand."

"Good." He inserts the key into the second door and pushes it open. "Place the book on the operating table. I have need of it there."

I slowly move toward the table and lay the book down. Some kind of experiment is taking place. There are three large bowls on the table, connected to one another by wires. Another wire travels from the third bowl to the cow's heart, which is on a silver platter.

Father takes down a black canvas apron from a

hook on the wall and ties it around his waist. "You can go now, Annabel."

I give him a brief curtsy and turn back to the stairwell. Just as I'm about to pull the door closed behind me, I hear a crash. Rushing back into the room, I find him on the floor surrounded by broken shards of glass. Knowing this is the second time I have seen him like this, I anticipate his anger.

But it never comes.

"Damn leg wants to be a bother," he says gruffly. There is embarrassment behind his words. Using the table to steady himself, he gets to his feet.

"Shall I fetch someone else to assist you, Father?" I ask.

"There is no one else, and I have squandered too much time already. You may stay until my tardy assistant arrives."

A wave of excitement sweeps over me, and I have to sternly remind myself to act like a lady. That's the only way to gain his respect. "Of course, Father," I say demurely. Waiting for his instructions, I clasp my hands together. I fear that if I do not, the excitement will overcome me.

"Take one of the aprons there from the hook. You

shall retrieve what I ask of you."

I nod and tie the apron tightly. My fingers are shaking, and I try to calm myself like I do during my morning meditations, by taking several deep breaths. This is my opportunity to show him I'm capable and proficient. Father opens the book I've placed on the table, and turns to a page near the back.

"I have need of the thin metal rod with the hook at the end of it," he says, nodding toward the tray of surgical implements. "Then we will begin."

I hand it to him, and he touches the heart gently with the rod.

But nothing happens.

He straightens and tries again. The result is the same. Touching the rod to the heart for a third time, he presses it deeply into the flesh. There is still no change. "I have the proper amounts of zinc and copper," he mutters. "The connection is strong."

He tinkers with the wire on the end of the rod. "The wire has been coated with salt water. . . ." He leans in to touch the page in front of him. "Yes," he says. "It's all right *here*. I don't understand what can be wrong."

I dare to voice my question. "What was supposed to have happened, Father?"

"Animal electricity." He toys with the wire again.

"Were this experiment a success, the spark would, in theory, make the heart beat again."

"Like the study of galvanism!" I say excitedly.

He turns to face me. "You've heard of it?"

"It was all the rage when Mother and I lived in England. I was too young, of course, to attend any of the showings, but I remember hearing about it. Luigi Galvani's nephew, Giovanni Aldini, would put on shows across Europe in which he would produce animal stimulation. When I grew older, I read about it."

"I believe his success to be doubtful. If his claims were real, then this should have worked. I followed his directions quite explicitly." Father prods the heart again as he speaks. "It's not just the heart," he mutters. "*That's* the problem. I know this. The brain is needed as well."

"What do you mean, the brain is needed?"

He suddenly looks up excitedly and throws the rod he's holding onto the table. "Go to that crate over there." He points at the shelf behind me. "And bring it here."

I hesitate momentarily. What will I see inside it?

"By all means, whenever you are ready," he says in exasperation.

Hurrying to the shelf, I do what he says. But I

cannot stop my sharp exhale when I look into the crate. A horse's head stares up at me. It's brown eyes wide and unblinking.

"Come, come now," he says. "You say you helped your mother in the village. Although this is an animal, there will not be much of a difference."

Human heads are not stored in crates with their eyes open and staring wide. But I know I cannot say what I'm thinking, so I carry the crate over to the table and set it down before him.

He lifts the head out of the crate and puts it directly onto the table. Even with all my doubts over whether or not my interest in medicine is abnormal, I cannot quell my curiosity.

"Bring me the cutting blade," Father says.

I find the one he wants and he places the blade at the back of the animal's head. Then he begins the arduous task of removing the skin and hair. When he hits bone, the noise it makes as he saws back and forth sets my teeth on edge. But I clasp my hands tightly together again, behind my back, and force myself to keep watching. If I turn away now, Father will no doubt see it as a sign of weakness. A sign that women cannot handle the study of medicine.

Once he's opened the horse's skull, he makes a few more cuts and then lifts the brain out. "Another tray is needed."

I search on the shelf behind me, but I cannot find one.

"To your left," he directs. "Just there."

Seizing an empty tray, I bring it to the table and place it beside him. The horse's head is within my line of sight, and I glance down at the floor, trying to avoid looking directly into its eyes.

"Sentimentality will keep women out of operating rooms forever," Father scoffs.

The comment stings, but I do my best not to react. "May I ask what it is you're going to do with the brain, Father?"

"I'm going to show you that in order to stimulate the heart, the brain is needed as well." His face lights up with anticipation. "That is truly where *life* comes from."

He carefully lays the brain on the tray and requests another wire. I hand it to him, and he links them together. The brain and the heart are now connected to each other, and the three bowls by their respective wires. I hold my breath as Father picks up the metal rod again. Then he touches the brain with it.

Suddenly, Father slams his hand on the table. "Another failure! I cannot understand what has gone wrong!"

He prods the brain again and again as he speaks until large holes appear, and the flesh begins to weaken. The prodding turns to stabbing.

His actions unsettle me. "Is there anything I can do, Father? Perhaps I can—"

His hand stills and he gives a deep sigh. "Just go. I have no further use of you."

Those words hurt more than his comment about being sentimental. Trying to tell myself that he is merely frustrated by his experiment, I hang up my apron and turn toward the door.

"Annabel." I glance back to see him following me, and my hope rises. "It was a mistake to let you help me," he says. "I hope you understand that. Women have no place in medicine or in science. It will not happen again."

"Yes, Father." My voice is a whisper.

"And tell that new watchman to go find my assistant. Otherwise, I'll need to find a new one. You are dismissed."

Before I can say anything more, the door shuts behind me and I'm left standing there alone in the dark. When the grating scratch of the key turning against the lock comes, it's a final death knell in the cold silence.

Thirteen

ook and Johanna are both in the kitchen when I return upstairs. Neither of them asks why I was down in the laboratory, but Cook casts a worried glance over at the door. "Father needed my assistance," I offer quietly. "Do either of you know where I can find Brahm?"

"He's in the stables with Jasper," Cook says. "What do you need him fer, miss?"

"Father's assistant is late and he has requested the new night watchman go find him."

Cook and Johanna share a look, and then Cook

says, "Johanna will find him, miss. No need fer you to be doing that."

Johanna agrees and hurries out into the courtyard while I take a seat at the worktable. "Do you know where Maddy is? Is she still cleaning the stained-glass windows?"

"She's in her room resting. Poor thing was as pale as a ghost, she said her stomach was upset an' she felt cold all over. I told her Johanna an' I could take care of preparing dinner."

Remembering the *khing* that I purchased at the marketplace, I get to my feet. "Will you put some water on to boil for tea, Cook? I have something that should make Maddy feel better."

She does as I ask while I go up to my room. The *khing* is still in my cloak pocket along with the handkerchief, and I reach for that as well. Hopefully, it will be a welcome distraction.

The tea is brewing when I reach the kitchen again, and Johanna has returned. I remove the *khing* from my pocket and cut a small section off, peeling away the outer bark and revealing the sweet flesh beneath. Dropping it into the teapot, I allow it to cook for several moments. "Fresh *khing* would be better, but this should work just as well."

"What is kring, miss?" Cook says.

I smile at her mispronunciation. "*Khing*, like the word *ring*, is an herb. I believe the shopkeeper at the apothecary told me it was called ginger here?"

"Ginger. Yes," Cook replies. "I've never had it in a tea, though."

"We used it often in Siam to relieve vapors, nausea, and fatigue. It should help Maddy feel better shortly."

They watch in silence as I strain the leaves and then flavor the tea with a small piece of sugar cube. In Siam, sliced oranges were used as flavoring. "Would you like to try some?" I ask. They nod, and I pour a cup for each of them.

Johanna takes a large sip of her tea. "Delicious, miss!"

Cook follows suit and then bobs her head. "I've never tasted anything like it!"

"If Maddy and I go back to the market again, I shall have to see if I can find *maphrao*—coconut. *Khing* is delicious paired with it." I glance around the kitchen. "Now, where might I find a tray so I can take this up to her?"

"I can take it, miss," Johanna says.

"Please, let me. I was hoping to spend a moment with her."

"Not to worry, miss." Cook finds a small silver tea tray and brings it over to me. "You go right ahead an' take it up yerself. Johanna will show you the way." Then she goes to the larder and comes back with biscuits and a small pot of cherry jam. "Her favorite," she says, adding those to the tray as well.

I follow Johanna up the staircase to the first floor. There are two doors on my left and two doors on my right. Johanna points to the right side of the hallway. "Our room is the last one down."

She leaves me behind, and I make my way to the second door on the right. Placing the tray on the floor, I knock gently and then pick it up again. A moment later, the door opens. Maddy's face peers out from behind it. Her eyes are red.

"I brought you some tea, Maddy," I say softly. "It's flavored with *kh* . . . ginger. From the market?"

"Oh, miss." She sniffles, and rubs her hand across her face. "You didn't have to do that."

"It will help you feel better. May I come in?"

Maddy glances behind her and then looks back to me again. "Miss . . . the room Johanna an' I share isn't very grand. It's not what yer used to."

"This whole house is not what I'm used to. Please, Maddy, don't be ashamed. The house Mother and I shared in Siam could fit twice over in my bedroom."

She pulls away from the door, and I start to think that perhaps she will not let me enter. But then she returns. "Yes, miss. Please come in."

Though the room is small and sparsely furnished, it's neat and tidy. There are two beds against the wall at my left and cheerful gingham curtains above a small window to my right. A chair sits beside the window with a pile of overturned crates beside it, stacked one on top of the other to create a makeshift table. Letters are scattered across the surface.

I gesture to the crates. "Is it all right if I put the tray down over there?"

She nods and moves forward to sweep the letters into a hasty pile. The "table" is shortened when she removes one of the crates and pushes it to the side. I put the tray down and she pulls out the chair for me to use. She takes a seat on the crate.

"Mother used to make this tea for me whenever I was feeling ill. It should help calm your stomach. The biscuits and jam are from Cook. She said they're your favorite."

She glances down. "Yes, miss."

Withdrawing the handkerchief from my pocket, I present it to her. "This is for you. A thank-you gift for being so kind to me."

Maddy looks up. Her eyes widen when she sees what's in my hand. "Fer me? But I've only been doing my job."

"That may be so, but you've also shown me the kindness of a friend. In Siam, we consider it an honor to give gifts that represent our appreciation and thanks."

"No one has ever given me a gift before."

"Then I hope you are pleased with it."

Tears spring to her eyes as she slowly takes the handkerchief. "How could I not be pleased grand? It's the one I've been admiring for ages!"

"Turn it over. It has your initials embroidered on it."

The look of delight on her face fills my heart near to bursting as she runs her finger over the embroidery. "It's the finest thing I have ever seen. Thank you, miss. Thank you!"

She stands to briefly embrace me, and I return her hug. "You are very welcome. Though I must ask one small favor of you in return."

"Anything, miss."

"Would you call me Annabel? It would mean the

world to me as your friend."

Maddy pulls back and bobs her head. Her eyes are sparkling. "You think of me as a friend?"

"I don't have very many," I confess. "Especially here in Philadelphia."

She blushes. "I would be pleased grand to be considered yer friend."

I squeeze her hand and give her a smile. At least for the moment, she seems to have forgotten whatever it was that upset her. "I should leave you to rest now. I do hope you feel better."

"Thank you, mi—Annabel," she corrects herself. "I will drink the tea you made me, too." She follows me to the door. "If I'm not able to finish my post here, I want you to know I've been pleased grand to be yer dressing maid," she says suddenly.

I turn to her. "Surely, you will not be fired simply because you were ill! I shall speak to Father and Grand-père. I will tell them—"

"Oh, no, miss." She shakes her head. "In case anything *should* happen, is all I mean."

"Is something wrong? Are you unhappy here?"

She's silent for a long moment. "What if you found out something. Something . . . you were ashamed to admit?"

"Like a secret you're forced to keep?"

She nods, and I reach for her hand. I'm all too familiar with those. "I would hope that it's not too great a burden for you. And if there's anything I can do to help, you have my word that I will."

She gives me another smile before pulling away. But it does not reach her eyes. As I descend the stairs to return to the kitchen, the image of her sad face, and her words of leaving, stay with me.

Fourteen

I wander the house the next afternoon, feeling melancholy and out of sorts, when a storm rolls in. Although there is no thunder, the rain is a constant companion. Slanting against the windows, casting dark shadows on the floor. I'm moody and restless—as dreary as the gray day outside—and I find myself returning to the library.

But the room is already occupied. Allan sits at the small table in front of the fireplace. He appears to be writing, and does not look up when I enter. His concentration is focused. A satchel is on the floor at his feet and a black work apron is still tied around his waist. His shirtsleeves have been rolled up, and there's a dark stain upon his neck.

I watch him silently. He shifts from one side of the chair to the other, murmuring softly to himself.

His brow furrows. "While I pondered weak and weary . . . ," he says. "Once upon a day so dreary." He scribbles something down on the paper before him. Then he pauses and frowns. "Deep into that darkness I stood peering . . ."

He abruptly stands, running his fingers through his hair. Several loose pieces escape the leather band at the nape of his neck, giving him a slightly wild look. The effect is not at all displeasing, and my heart starts to beat rapidly.

"For you came tapping." He begins pacing in front of the fire. "Tapping, tapping, tapping. Tapping and rapping at my chamber door! You are always rapping at my chamber door!"

I draw in a sudden breath.

He turns, and his eyes meet mine. "Miss Lee . . . I did not expect anyone to be here." He removes his apron and begins to roll down his shirtsleeves.

"I did not think anyone else would be here either.

I'm sorry to interrupt you." I hope my voice is steady. The sight of his bare arms is distracting.

"No apology is necessary. Your presence could never be an interruption." He motions to the chair opposite the one he had been occupying. "Would you care to join me? My writing is not going as well as I'd hoped. I'm in need of inspiration."

"Were you working on something new?" I take a seat and place my hands on the table. "I thought you would be with Father in his laboratory this afternoon." I wonder if Father has mentioned that I was his assistant yesterday.

"We are . . . taking a short respite. Your father was unhappy with our progress and wanted some time to gather his thoughts. Since I had a free moment, I stole away."

"And you came here for inspiration? I suppose I shouldn't be surprised, since you're a lover of words."

I blush when I hear the word *lover* come out of my mouth.

He arches one eyebrow at me. "I'm a lover of beauty as well, and it seems I've made the right decision to come here, after all. Today, I find both of my inspirations fulfilled."

My face grows even warmer, and I look down again. *He considers me beautiful?* "I am not fair skinned," I protest. "My hands are rough, and sun-worn. My eyes are not light, my hair is not pale. I—"

He reaches out and gently touches the back of my hand. His hand lingers there.

My heart pounds, and all of Mrs. Tusk's lessons collide in my head. I glance at the bookshelves beside us. "I came looking for a book to pass the time. I was feeling restless, and the storm drove me to wander. Is there one you would suggest?"

Allan pulls his hand back, and briskly clears his throat. "I usually find it's during those moments when I'm inspired the most. Restlessness has led to many of the poems for my first book."

"First book?" I look shyly up at him. "Are you planning to write more?"

"Dozens. Hundreds. I aim to be one of the most admired writers in all of history. I have already been critiqued by Washington Irving." His eyes shine with pride. "Have you heard of him? I shall have to show you the letter he wrote to me!"

"I fear I have not. We did not have many books to read in Siam."

"He is a much-praised American writer and is very well known. His most famous work has been *The Sketch Book of Geoffrey Crayon, Gent.* But already at half his age, I will have my first book published. Though lately . . ." He looks over my shoulder, and his gaze grows distant. As though he's lost in something far beyond me. "Lately, I've felt . . ."

"Felt what, Allan?"

His attention returns to me. "Have you ever felt like a story was inside you, but you couldn't do it justice? Almost as though some *other* part of you needed to write it down? Whether you could not find the inspiration, or the words, or the atmosphere, or the setting . . . It's as if there were something standing in your way, stopping you, and only this other piece of you could understand whatever it was?"

"Sometimes, I'm unsure of how to express my feelings." My face grows warm as I think how this applies not only to my own writing, but to my feelings for him. "My words do not seem to accurately capture the moment and all that it encompasses."

"Exactly!" Allan grips the edge of the table. "I have started something different. Something darker than anything I've ever written before. A study on the effects of death, and the shadows her dark pallor casts on all of us when murder is involved. Although I can *see* the story inside my head, the words come to me only in rare moments. I have tried . . ." He stops and shakes his head. "I've tried many things to write when I wish to, but the words will not come. And then, just when I'm no longer thinking about it, I find that I *have* written parts of this story. I find these words written in the oddest places, but try as hard as I might, I cannot recreate them."

His words draw me in, and suddenly I find myself leaning toward him, putting my hand on top of his. "Inspiration is fickle, Allan, but you have a true talent. You will find your way."

"I have been inspired"—he turns his hand so that his palm is touching mine—"every time I see you." His hand is large, and I can feel the roughness of his skin as he entwines his fingers with my own. It seems as though every heartbeat, pulsing within my veins, echoes between us. Slowly, he leans in closer. With his free hand, he traces a curl that has fallen loose down my shoulder.

"So beautiful," he whispers.

I'm afraid to draw a breath.

His hand moves to my cheek and I feel dizzy. The

experience is strange and frightening and wonderful. As I part my lips to breathe, I find that I want to draw him in even closer. And, as if by some unspoken magic, he leans in.

And then he kisses me.

His mouth tastes like cherries, with just a hint of the brandy Grand-père gave to me, and his lips are so warm I wonder if they'll burn me. He kisses me delicately at first, as the butterflies in my chest fly faster and the rain turns fierce, pounding against the windows with a relentless onslaught of wind and fury. We have already crossed the bounds of propriety. But I'm drawn helplessly toward him for more.

His lips move to my ear, leaving a white-hot trail on my skin. "Annabel," he breathes, nipping at my earlobe. The pain is exquisite. I never want it to end. My breath quickens, and it feels as if I'm drowning again beneath the water, like when we first met. Lost under the waves that crash over my head and drag me under, even as I struggle to break through the surface. I cannot think for this mad wanting.

He pulls away, and I want to cry out—to beg him not to leave. But he turns his attention to my throat, and I'm satisfied again. He moves slowly toward the collar of my dress, when a flare of panic seizes me.

He pushes aside my scarf.

"No," I gasp, moving away. My stays are making it impossible to breathe.

He stands abruptly. "I have forgotten myself. I'm sorry. Forgive me, it will not happen again."

"No, Allan . . ." I straighten my scarf and then touch the combs in my hair. They are loose, and I'm sure I must look disheveled. I can hear Mrs. Tusk's voice in my head again, speaking of proper etiquette and reputation. "There is nothing to forgive. I was just overwhelmed. It was . . . I did not mean to push you away."

"No?"

He waits expectantly.

"No," I whisper.

He pulls me to my feet and holds me close. The sensation make my heart pound frantically. My body is pressed against his.

"You have haunted my dreams. My waking hours. Every moment in between," he says.

I stare up at him, lost in the darkness of his eyes.

He lowers his mouth to mine, and just before he steals my breath again, he echoes my thoughts. "I am lost in you."

Fifteen

I request dinner in my room that evening, telling Cook I'm not feeling well. I cannot face Father or Grand-père after spending the afternoon with Allan. My face will surely betray every thought I have of him. And, truthfully, although I'm not feeling ill in the traditional sense, a mad fever races through my bones. Though we parted only hours ago, I long to see him again.

My body grows hot as I sit at my desk and relive his kisses. Glancing down at my arm, I trace the path that his lips took. Every finger, every bone, down the soft inner part of my wrist where he lingered . . .

And then I think of where *my* fingers traveled. How I freed his hair from the band at his neck and ran my hands through the soft, silken strands. It created a dark halo around us as he rested his forehead on mine. I could see myself reflected in his eyes, and the picture of wild abandon that I presented there shocked me. My lips were swollen, eyes wide, hair loose around my shoulders. He lifted one hand and tangled his fingers in my curls, dragging in a ragged breath and we spent a long moment in silence.

I close my eyes and then open them again, leaning forward to peer into the looking glass. *Do I look any different? Will anyone take one glance at me and see that I'm his?*

But the glass reflects only my normal self. My lips are no longer swollen, my cheeks are no longer red. The only thing changed are my eyes. . . . Something deeper shines out from them now. A knowledge that was not there before.

❧ ❧ ❧

Johanna helps me undress for bed since Maddy is still ill, and I quickly climb beneath the covers. I can feel myself drifting off before she even leaves the room, and I mumble a good night. When my dreams suddenly turn to someone shaking my shoulder, I try to ignore the intrusion.

"Miss! Please wake up, miss. I need yer help," a voice whispers urgently in my ear.

I frown, and burrow deeper beneath the covers.

"Miss, please, wake up. Miss . . . *Annabel*!"

My name is enough to rouse me from my slumber, and I open my eyes. Maddy's frightened face is bent down close to mine, a trembling candle between us. Her whole body is shaking. "Maddy? What is it?"

She bites her lips and tears fill her eyes. "I need yer help. I know I should not be asking, but I have no one else. She's hurt bad, an' I don't know what to do. Since you helped Johanna, I thought maybe you could help me, too."

A sense of calm immediately comes over me. Mother always told me that, in a time of panic, a clear head is necessary.

"What do you need, Maddy?" I climb out of bed and hurry across the room to the armoire. Ignoring the corset and petticoat, I reach for my traveling dress and put it on directly over my shift. The tone of her voice tells me I'm needed too urgently to worry about propriety. I pull out my bedroom slippers and put those on as well.

"It's Mama. She's hurt an' needs help."

"Of course. Where is she?"

"At our house near the marketplace."

"Let me stop by the kitchen for some supplies, and then we can be on our way."

Maddy nods and takes my hand, leading me down the back staircase. Her hand is like ice. That she took mine without hesitation must mean she is even more worried than she's let on. Once I have twine and a needle, a pair of scissors, the nettle-and-licorice salve, and linen for bandages, we exit through the kitchen door and go through the gate leading from Father's courtyard to the street.

As we walk, I come to the realization that I'm about to openly defy Father. Only yesterday he told me he still thinks medicine has no place for women . . .

I quicken my pace. No matter what he says, I will not allow Maddy's mother to go without medical aid.

We hurry on through the dark. Without Maddy by my side, I would surely lose my way. She takes me down narrow alleys where the row houses grow smaller and smaller until we come to a tall, skinny one. As we enter, there are several flights of stairs to climb. On the fifth floor, Maddy stops at the first door and pulls out a key. The room beyond is small and poorly lit. The only light comes from two stubby candles stuck on tin plates, glowing in melted puddles of wax.

A cough comes from behind a curtain on my left, and I see dirty feet hanging from the edge of a cot. "Is that her?" I ask.

Maddy nods and pulls back the curtain.

At first, I see nothing more than a pile of blankets. I let my eyes adjust to the semi-darkness as Maddy holds up one of the tin plates bearing a candle. Then the blankets move. A woman's face peers up at me, and I stifle my gasp.

Sharp cheekbones jut out beneath sunken eye sockets. There is dried blood at the corners of her mouth, and a fresh bruise stretches across her jaw. Her skin is tinged with the pallor of malnutrition. She holds out a gnarled hand to me and her mouth opens in a silent scream.

"Be calm," I say gently. "I'm a friend of Maddy's. She brought me here to help you." I hold very still and make sure my tone is low and soothing. "My name is Annabel."

Maddy comes closer. "It's true, Mama." Leaning down, she gently takes her mother's hand. "She's a healer. Let her have a look at yer leg now. Please?"

Maddy's mother shrinks back. She does not have enough strength to resist the request, though she is clearly terrified.

"My own mother was a healer, too." I move slowly toward the cot. It is low to the ground, so I sit on the floor. "She taught me everything she knew." I glance quickly at the bottom of the blanket and see a large black stain. My heart beats faster at the sight. I must convince her to allow me to see what has happened.

But in her fear, she pulls herself almost off the edge of the cot to get away from me. Her eyes are wide and scared.

I start humming softly, and then find the words to the song Mother used to sing. "*Oh, the oak and the ash and the bonny birken tree. They flourish at home in her own country. A north country maiden up to London had strayed, although with her nature it did not agree. She wept and she sighed, and so bitterly she cried: I wish once again, in the north I could be.*"

Maddy's mother's lips start to move and she forms the words along with me. "*Oh, the oak and the ash and the bonny birken tree. They flourish at home in her own country. . . ."*

We sing the rest, and I move my hand to her forehead. Gray hair clings to her bare scalp in clumps. I don't know what's happened to this poor woman, but she has not known an easy life. Her eyes start to drift closed. "I'm going to remove the blankets now," I say softly. "I won't do anything more than look, though, I promise."

I glance at Maddy and she nods her agreement. She starts humming, and I'm thankful she can help keep her mother distracted. I lift up the blanket. It's stiff with dried blood, and smells like putrefaction. I steel myself for what I'm going to find.

When the leg is fully revealed, it's even worse than I imagined. The flesh is rotting. A strip of skin at least six inches wide is missing from the entire length of her lower limb, knee to foot. If it were a simple cut, I could stitch the edges of the wound together. But there isn't enough skin to do that. I've never seen anything like this before.

I look at Maddy, and she must be able to tell how helpless I'm feeling.

"I'm going to get you some water, Mama," she says,

withdrawing her hand. "I'll just be right over here."

Her mother gives no sign that she understands what Maddy is saying. The only indication that she's still alive is the slow rise and fall of her chest. I follow behind Maddy, and keep my voice low. "I would try to close the wound, but it's so large and there is so little flesh left. . . ." I shake my head in frustration.

Maddy wrings her hands. "I did not know how bad it was. I only just found out. My brother wrote me an' told me he came home to her like this."

"Oh, Maddy . . . Her wound should have been seen to at least a week past."

Maddy's hand-wringing continues, and she worries her lip. I put my hand on top of hers. *Is this what she meant about losing her mother?*

"What happened?" I ask.

"She's touched. It started when I was ten. We all tried to keep an eye on her. Me an' my brothers an' sisters. But Mama was found wandering the streets one day an' committed to Pennsylvania Hospital. To the women's insane ward."

"And she was . . . released?" I cannot bring myself to ask if she escaped.

Maddy nods. "Last week. They said she was cured.

She's been here on her own an' I just found out. That's why I was so upset, Miss Annabel. Why I was ashamed."

There is no delicate way to ask my next question. "Did she do this to . . . herself?"

Maddy nods again, miserably. "When I was little, Mama thought bugs were crawling beneath her skin, an' she would tear off great bloody chunks to get at them."

How difficult it must be to go through life having to take care of your mother instead of having her take care of you. "I'll clean the wound and apply some salve. Then we'll cover the injury and try to keep it dry."

While I ready my supplies, Maddy fetches a glass of water. When I'm ready, she props her mother's head upon her shoulder and helps her take a sip. "I'll try to be quick," I say.

Thankfully, luck is on my side, and the wound is easy to clean. It's messy work, though, and I have to keep exchanging dirty rags for fresh ones. When there are no more signs of putrefaction, I dress the wound with a clean bandage.

Standing wearily, I wash my hands in a bucket that serves as a sink. "That's all I can do for now. The rest is up to God." My back is sore and my legs ache from sitting for so long.

Maddy joins me a moment later, her face showing relief. "Mama's sleeping."

"Good. Rest will help her heal quickly."

"Miss, I—"

"Annabel."

She blushes and looks down.

"You mustn't thank me, if that's what you're thinking, Maddy. You're my friend and you had a need. I wouldn't be acting as *your* friend if I didn't help when I could."

She opens her mouth to say something more, but then simply nods. Her shoulders slump. She looks exhausted.

I press the pot of salve and the rest of the bandages into her hands. "Remember, just as I told Johanna, after the first three days, the bandages need to be changed and new salve applied. Keep an eye on the edges of the wound for discoloration."

Maddy bobs her head and takes the supplies, placing them on the floor next to the cot. "I'll be sure to do as you say, Miss Annabel." Then she returns to me. "We should be getting back to yer father's house now."

"I'm glad you'll be with me, Maddy. I don't think I can find my way home in the dark."

Maddy glances over at a grimy window above the bucket. The window is so small, I had not noticed it was there. "It's not dark out anymore. There's daylight."

My heart sinks as I look over and see this is true. Morning has come.

And I've been out all night.

Sixteen

We race through the streets, trying to get back to Father's house before we're missed. The morning air is crisp and cool with a light covering of fog on the ground, and I rub my hands together to try to warm them. We're almost there when, rounding a corner, I stumble on a loose stone. Hands reach out to catch me before I fall, and I look up to see a familiar face.

"Edgar."

He helps me regain my footing, though he wears a sly expression. "My, my, my. Since your father had an early morning errand, I know why *I'm* out and about at such an ungodly hour, but what about *you*?" He glances over at Maddy. "Have you not heard there's a murderer on the loose?"

I draw away from him. "My maid needed my help."

"Did she? And what assistance did she require?"

Maddy takes a protective step in front of me. "That's none of your concern."

"Mmmm-hmm." Edgar looks at Maddy, and then back to me. When his eyes shift lower, I pull the edges of my dress tightly around me. Not only am I without a coat, but my laces are still open in the back. I shiver uncontrollably as the morning air hits the thin material.

Edgar makes an aggravated sound, and then removes his overcoat. He roughly drapes it around my shoulders. "Here. Take this."

Before I can object, he is striding away from me, his cane tapping furiously as he heads in the direction from which Maddy and I just came. I turn to face Maddy. She appears as surprised as I am.

"Edgar Poe acting like a gentleman," she says solemnly. "I never thought I'd live to see the day." Her shocked reverie lasts a moment longer, and then she blinks. Tugging on my hand, she pulls me forward. "We need to go, miss. Now."

We pass through the gate and cross the courtyard, creeping quietly into the kitchen. Cook and Johanna are preparing breakfast and they give us questioning looks, but Maddy holds one finger up to her mouth in a silent request. They nod and go back to their tasks. We're almost to the kitchen stairs, when the door from the dining room suddenly opens.

"I have repeatedly asked that the paper be waiting for me in the morning," Father says loudly as he enters the room. "Where is that serving girl? I am in need of some coffee and—"

He halts when he sees us. Moments later, Grand-père follows.

"Well . . . ," Grand-père says. He is clearly at a loss for words. "Well . . ."

Father does not say anything at all.

Aware of how shocking I must appear, given the fact that I'm barely dressed and wearing a gentleman's overcoat, I try to compose myself. "There was an emergency. My help was needed," is all I can manage.

"Beggin' yer pardon, sir," Maddy says. She looks down at the ground. "Miss Annabel was with my mother. She hurt herself."

A dark look of disbelief shadows Father's face. He ignores Maddy and glares at me. "You were practicing medicine?"

Every word is as sharp as a razor.

"Yes."

"After I forbade it?"

"Yes."

He glances down at his left cuff and adjusts it. "I see."

"Why don't we take this conversation into the dining room?" Grand-père suggests.

"I don't see why," Father rebuts. "I—"

"Not in front of the servants, Markus." Grand-père turns back to the dining room, and Father reluctantly follows. Maddy glances at me, and I shake my head. I know she wants to help, but I've made my choice. I will deal with the consequences, whatever they may be.

"What was she thinking?" I hear Father saying as I enter the dining room. "Roaming the streets at night . . . There will be talk if anyone has seen her. I do not need unwanted attention drawn to this house. Idle gossip already abounds."

"We must remember that she's not yet used to our ways, Markus," Grand-père replies. "Give her time."

An immense feeling of love floods through my heart for Grand-père. He always tries to understand me. "My sincerest apologies for offending you, Father," I say in a rush. "I merely offered my assistance to someone who had need of medical aid."

"If you were *merely* offering your medical services— something which I have not only forbidden you to do but that is also illegal without a license—why are you wearing a gentleman's coat? Were your services rendered to *him* as well?"

I fight not to blush, and try to keep my voice steady. "No, Father. I only helped Maddy's mother. She's an aging woman in poor health, and I bandaged a wound she had suffered. Surely, that is not against the law?"

"Of course putting a bandage on a wound is not against the law," Father scoffs. "The point is that I forbade you from doing anything of the sort."

"I'm sure Annabel was simply trying to be helpful," Grand-père says.

"Then how did she end up wearing a gentleman's coat?" Father turns his sharp gaze back toward me.

My hands are growing slick, the room seems overly warm. "It was an act of kindness, Father. It was cold out, and I forgot my own coat. Your assistant, Edgar, gave me his as he passed by."

"An act of kindness?" He lets out a sharp laugh and then turns on his heel, silently dismissing me. "There is nothing kind about him."

※   ※   ※

I don't eat breakfast, returning to my room instead, so I can gather my composure before my morning lessons. Mrs. Tusk will be expecting me in the sitting room at eight o'clock. My stomach tightens as I do my meditations. *Please watch over me, Mother, and let my lessons with Mrs. Tusk go smoothly.*

After my quarrel with Father, I cannot bear the thought of having anyone else upset with me.

I'm in the middle of washing my face, when there's a knock at the door. "Come in," I call out.

Maddy enters. She's silent as she helps me get dressed. When I turn back around to face her, her fingers lock together nervously. "I felt awfully bad when we came upon the Master an' Grandmaster this morning, Miss Annabel. I did not mean for trouble to come to you."

"It was my choice to help your mother, and it's one I would gladly make again. Do not be concerned."

"Thank you fer helping me," she says earnestly. "I was sick to my soul with worry about what to do. If you wouldn't've come . . ." Maddy shakes her head. "I never could've paid a doctor myself."

"Let's hope what I did will be enough. I'm not a doctor yet."

"It's more than I could've done on my own," she replies. "That has to count for something."

She nods eagerly, and I smile at her. But my smile falters. "Do you think . . . do you think I'm abnormal because of my interest in medicine? Perhaps it is not natural. Perhaps it would be better if only men were doctors and—"

"If only men were to be int'rested in such things, we would surely be in a sorry place," she interrupts. "You have a good an' kind heart. There is nothing abnormal about that. *Nothing*."

"But Father thinks it is unseemly."

"Forgive me, but the Master also thinks the sun rises up ev'ry day just for him." She lets out a short laugh, and then her face turns serious. "You have a gift, Annabel, an' surely it would be more of a spite to God's face to not use the gift he gave you than to not follow yer father's decree."

"You're right, Maddy. I should not let him make such a decision for me."

She blushes and touches something at her neck. When she moves her hand away, I see a string around her throat.

I peer closer at it. "What's that, Maddy?"

She pulls the string from beneath her collar, drawing out a tarnished oval locket. "Mama gave me this long ago." Her face is filled with happiness as she gazes down at it. "I wanted to wear it today to keep her close." She holds the locket out for me to see, and then places it next to her heart once more.

"It's beautiful, Maddy. I'm sure you treasure it." Turning toward the bed, I lift my pillow and remove the zodiac book. "I do the same thing with a book my mother gave me. I carry it with me so I'll never be alone."

Maddy blinks rapidly and looks away. When she's regained her composure, she says, "Come an' take a seat at the desk now, miss. Let's finish yer toilet before I go all soft in the eyes."

🌸 🌸 🌸

My lessons with Mrs. Tusk go very well, and she even offers me a begrudging compliment for my recitation of the French alphabet. When we stop for lunch, Maddy tells me that a message from Madame LaFleur has just been received.

"Yer dresses are ready earlier than Madame thought," she says. "They are to be delivered tomorrow."

"Would it be improper for me to pick the dresses up, rather than waiting for them to be delivered? I long to be free of this gown I've been wearing ever since I stepped foot off the ship from Siam."

"Not if you send yer maid," she says with a smile.

"May I go with you? I hoped to stop at the apothecary again to see if they have coconuts."

"Of course, Miss Annabel."

As soon as Mrs. Tusk has finished our afternoon lessons, and taken her leave, I find Maddy and we set out for the marketplace. But when we reach Madame LaFleur's shop, I hesitate. I remember what she said about associating with Father. Will she be unhappy to see me, as well? What if she turns me away?

"Are you sure she will not be offended by the fact

that I did not wait for the wardrobe to be delivered?" I ask.

"Servants often fetch deliveries," Maddy explains. "I'll tell Madame you simply could not wait another moment to see her handiwork. She'll be pleased grand by that."

"As long as you're sure . . . ?"

Maddy nods and enters Madame LaFleur's shop. She returns moments later with several packages wrapped in brown paper tied neatly with string. I offer to help her carry them, but she gives me a stern look. "Yer place," she reminds me.

"Of course," I say ruefully. "How could I forget?" We cross the street to the apothecary, and a woman behind the counter greets us. I look to see if there are any coconuts available, but unfortunately, there are none to be found. Something else on the shelf catches my eye, though. "You have angel trumpet?"

The woman glances at me apologetically. "Can you point to what you're referring to?"

I gesture to the white, bell-shaped flower. I recognize it from home. It's highly poisonous, and coming into contact with the blooms can cause a deathlike sleep.

"My apologies, I'm not familiar with everything in our shipments. My husband is normally the one who . . ." She grows flustered. ". . . who deals with such things."

"Oh, are you Mrs. Williams?" I ask.

She nods, but looks down at the floor.

"Mr. Williams was very helpful the last time I came in. I hope he's not ill." She shakes her head and tears fill her eyes, but she does not say anything more. I share a look with Maddy and then briefly bow to Mrs. Williams. "I do not see anything I wish to purchase today. Thank you for your time."

She mumbles a soft reply as Maddy and I leave the shop behind. I don't have a chance to ask Maddy what she thought of such strange behavior, though, because a young boy is yelling in the streets. Several people have paused to listen, while a cap at his feet collects spare coins.

"Murder's been committed!" he calls. "Murder most foul! Body found missing the heart!"

"Who is that?" I ask Maddy.

"A news crier. Says what's happened before they can print up the news."

Someone next to me shouts that the information is

too vulgar for the ears of women and children, while the person beside him shouts for more: "Missing the heart? What's happened to it?"

"It was found beneath the floorboards of an empty house," the crier replies.

"When did it happen?" someone else yells.

"Early this morning," he answers back. "The gent worked at this very marketplace—at the apothecary!"

The crowd goes silent, but my heartbeat is suddenly echoing loudly in my ears. *It cannot be. It must not be . . .*

"Mr. Williams," the crier says. "It was Mr. Williams."

Seventeen

Maddy and I are made somber by the news from the market, and when we arrive home, she silently unwraps the packages. I should be thrilled by the sight of the dresses, but I'm consumed with troubled thoughts. So much has happened with Father that I'd almost forgotten there is a murderer on the streets. Now to hear poor Mr. Williams is one of the victims . . .

Telling Maddy that I'm going for a walk, I slip down the back staircase and out into the courtyard. The air is cool, and the sun is rapidly sinking behind clouds. The door on the far side of the courtyard stands open, and I see Brahm coming through it from the alleyway beyond.

He stops for a moment, and turns to speak to someone behind him. Then Father awkwardly steps through the door. He hands Brahm a piece of paper, and they speak again before Brahm nods and goes back through the door. Father continues across the courtyeard. Before he can see me, I move quickly back into the kitchen.

I wait on the staircase as he enters, thumping across the floor. I hear the sound of keys dropping and a muttered curse, followed by a door opening and closing. He must have gone down to his laboratory.

I leave my hiding spot, wondering if Brahm was one of the men I saw making a delivery for Father in the dead of night. Was it the horse's head? Is that how Father receives the strange specimens he keeps in jars?

The sound of voices interrupts my thoughts, and I head toward the great room as I hear Maddy greeting someone at the door. I quicken my pace when I hear Allan's voice returning her greeting. He's dressed in a white shirt again, and dark pants. He smiles when he seems me, then bows and takes my hand.

Maddy watches our exchange with a hint of a smile,

then discreetly excuses herself. Allan gently touches my cheek.

"Is something the matter?" he asks. Concern fills his eyes. "You look upset."

"I was with Maddy at the market when there was news of another murder. The victim was Mr. Williams, the apothecary owner. I'd just spoken with him a few days ago."

His finger slides down to my chin, and he lifts my face. "I'm sorry, Annabel. I wish I could take this pain from you."

I stare into his eyes for just a moment before he claims my mouth with his own. His fingers move down to my shoulders, across my rib cage, and wrap around my waist.

Even through the thick fabric of my dress, I can feel his touch as if there is nothing between us. A shiver runs through me. My breath is stolen again and again, until he finally breaks away. "Your father expects me. I must go."

His breathing is ragged. I can feel his heart pounding.

I stand on tiptoe to wrap my arms around his neck.

"Annabel . . ." He breathes my name and, with a

groan, gives in and frames my face with his hands. They are rough against my skin, but the feeling of being connected to him, of feeling this unnamed *something* that burns like fire between us, makes me long for more. Our lips meet one last time and then I relent, pulling back so he may take his leave and go to Father.

"I'm sorry to have kept you." I touch my scarf, and then place my hands on my cheeks. They are so very warm.

His collar is crooked and his left shirtsleeve has come unbuttoned. He sets himself to rights, and I give him a shy smile as he says, "I would gladly miss a thousand appointments for more time with you." He traces my cheek. "I'll have a break tomorrow morning. Can I persuade you to take a stroll in the courtyard to watch the sunrise?"

"I would not miss it for the world."

Allan catches my fingers and gives my hand a quick kiss. "Tomorrow morning at seven fifteen, then. I'll see you in the—"

He's suddenly interrupted by a loud banging at the front door. It continues until he strides over and opens it.

A red-faced Mrs. Tusk stands on the stoop outside,

one fist still raised. Her hair has completely escaped the tidy bun she normally wears, but she doesn't seem to have noticed. A folded sheet of paper is in her hand and she waves it angrily. "Is he home?" she demands, pushing her way in. "Where is he? I must speak with the master of the house right now."

"Now see here, madam," Allan says. "You can't just come barging in like this. You will have to make an appointment."

Mrs. Tusk thrusts the paper at Allan. "*This* guarantees my appointment."

He takes the paper and scans it. "This is no invitation, madam. This is a dismissal. I believe the intent is clear—you will have to leave."

"I will *not* leave!" She tries to push past Allan, but he stands his ground. "He thinks he can send me this note, does he?" she mutters. "I'll make sure Williams hears of this! We will not be cut out."

Suddenly, she pulls herself up to her full height and turns her attention toward me. "Is this your doing? Did you have a part in my dismissal?" She does not wait for my answer. "I heard talk of this house, they warned me I would regret coming here. But I was forced into this position. To think that I have fallen so low as to have to teach someone with *your* shameful upbringing . . ." She shakes her head. "Here's a message you can give to your father from me, you . . . you . . ."

Before I can react, her hand whips forward and her palm leaves its outline against my cheek. "Illegitimate heathen!"

For a moment, I am sorely tempted to slap her right back. But then Allan grips her by the shoulders. "You are very lucky you are a woman, madam," he says furiously. He carries her backward through the door and deposits her unceremoniously onto the street. "Were you a man, I would give you the comeuppance you so justly deserve."

I can still hear Mrs. Tusk's shouting outside as Allan returns. Shutting the door firmly behind him, he sweeps me off my feet and carries me into the kitchen. "Cook!" he yells. "Johanna! Maddy!"

"You don't have to carry me," I protest. "I am not harmed." But I grip the back of his shoulders tightly, feeling delicate in his arms. Perhaps I should make the most of such a situation.

"You *are* harmed." Anger fills his eyes as he looks down at me. "I can see the mark that beastly woman left on you."

Cook and Johanna come running. They gasp when they catch sight of me. "What happened?" Johanna asks.

"A visit from Mrs. Tusk," Allan replies. "She misplaced her manners, so I showed her to the door."

"Master Allan!" Cook huffs. She's out of breath. "It's not proper fer you to be so close."

"I am only holding her," Allan says. "Not ravaging her."

Cook directs Allan to set me down by the fireplace and hurries over to the potato bin. When she returns, she carries a large knife and a potato, which she sets on the chopping block. She slices it in half and hands me a piece. "Fer the swelling. We don't want the master to think you was in a tussle, now, do we?"

Johanna brings me a damp cloth and gently wipes my face. The coolness is soothing, and I hold the potato to my cheek. Allan watches them fussing over me, then casts a glance at the door to Father's laboratory.

"Go," I tell him. "I am well cared for here."

But he still looks unsure.

"*Go*," I say again. "You do not want to be late. It would make Father unhappy."

Leaning down, he gently kisses my unblemished cheek. "Tomorrow morning in the courtyard, seven fifteen," he whispers.

His lips are so close that if I were to turn my head, they would touch mine. But I'm aware that we are not alone, so I simply nod and try not to blush.

"Take good care of her," he says to Cook and Johanna.

"Don't you worry none, Master Allan," Cook says. "Our young miss will be right as rain with us watching over her."

With one final long look at me, Allan strides over to the fireplace and then disappears behind the door that will take him down to my father's laboratory.

❀　❀　❀

I sit with Cook and Johanna until I find myself discreetly hiding several yawns, and then slip upstairs to my bedroom for a short rest before dinner. When I return to the dining room, the imprint from Mrs. Tusk's hand has faded from my face and I'm feeling greatly refreshed.

Father does not join us at the table again, but I'm

relieved by his absence. Although I'm curious as to why he's dismissed Mrs. Tusk; if he were here, I would not be able to stop myself from asking him about it. And with his ever changing moods, it would surely displease him.

After dinner, I quickly excuse myself and return to my room. When I reach my door, however, it's slightly ajar. I hear the sound of water splashing, and I open it to find Maddy standing next to a gleaming copper bathing tub. Steam rises around her shoulders, and a curl has worked its way free of her plaited hair. But her face is beaming with a jubilant smile.

"Maddy!" I step into the room. "What is this?"

"Cook told me what happened with that horrible woman." She casts a quick glance at my cheek and then looks away. "I never should've left you an' Master Allan alone. I'll go back to the house an' retrieve the salve you left fer Mama. That will help."

"Oh, no, Maddy, she needs it more than I do. I'll be fully healed by tomorrow. And if you had not left Allan and me alone ..." My cheeks warm.

Her crooked grin returns. "I swear, Miss Annabel, I thought I heard Cook calling fer me."

I return her smile and glance over at the tub again.

It's been *ages* since I've had a bath. And never in a tub as big as the one that's before me now.

"We wanted to surprise you," Maddy says, catching my look of longing. "Cook an' Johanna an' me. Cook hauled the tub up, an' me an' Johanna took turns carrying the water."

They did this for me? I give her the biggest smile I have and then hug her. "Thank you. And please give Cook and Johanna my thanks, as well."

Maddy returns my hug, but wiggles out of it a moment later. "Let's get you undressed now. Water's getting cold." Quickly undoing my laces, she hangs my dress in the armoire. "I'll leave you in peace now. Enjoy yer bath."

I quickly remove the last of my undergarments as soon as the door has shut behind her. The feeling is deliciously freeing. Balancing on the edge of the tub, I put the towel on the floor beside me and step carefully into the water. A satisfied sigh escapes me. It truly is a wonderful feeling. The water rises higher, edging closer to my neck, and then I realize that I'm still wearing my scarf.

I glance quickly around the room. Mother told me never to take it off. But I'm completely alone here.

Gripping the edges of the tub, I pull myself to a sitting position and slowly unwind the linen scarf. It falls to the floor. I slide back under the water until my ears are covered, and I close my eyes. It feels as if all of my cares are floating away.

But a sudden vibration makes me open my eyes again. I lift my head to see Maddy entering the room, and water streams in every direction as I hastily sit up. There is no time to reach for my scarf, so I use my hands to try to shield myself from her.

I'm not worried about my modesty. I'm worried about the scars.

A sliver of soap is cradled in Maddy's cupped hands, but she comes to a halt when she sees me. Her eyes trace the grotesque patchwork covering the upper part of my chest and neck. Although I have not looked at them in many years, I know the scars are still as dark and ugly as the first time I saw them when I was very young.

The true reason I never take off my scarf is now on full display.

Maddy comes over to the edge of the tub, but doesn't stare. "I forgot to leave the soap. Would you like me to help you wash yer hair?"

I can hardly believe she's not shrinking back in fear, or fleeing from disgust. Mother told me the scars came from an operation when I was a baby, but that we were never to speak of it. I felt such shame growing up with them. But now Maddy is acting as if she does not see them at all.

"You're not afraid of me?" I say unbelievingly.

"Why should I be?"

"Because I'm a monster. My skin is disfigured, and I'm hideous to look at."

"Yer not a monster. Yer my friend."

Her simple words are so genuine. I bow my head, throat thick with tears. "I . . . would be truly grateful if you helped me wash my hair, Maddy. No one has ever offered before."

She reaches into the tub and lathers up the soap. Her hands are gentle as she scrubs my hair, and then she tells me to close my eyes as she scoops water over my head to rinse away the bubbles. When she tells me I can open my eyes again, and I notice the string that held her locket is no longer around her neck.

"What happened to your necklace, Maddy?" I ask.

She glances down and absentmindedly toys with her collar. "It's safe in the kitchen. I took it off while I hauled the water fer the tub." She places the soap on the floor within my reach and turns to leave.

But by the door, she pauses. "I will tell no one yer secret, Miss Annabel. It's safe with me. I promise."

And as the door shuts quietly behind her, I cannot stop myself from thinking that now there's one more secret for this house to keep.

Eighteen

I wake before the sun rises the next morning. Climbing out of bed, I pull on my red silk robe and reach for my scarf. But instead of wrapping it around my neck, I sit and stare at it. Pondering Maddy's reaction to my scars—how she now knows the secret I have kept for so many years.

Gathering the scarf, I walk over to the looking glass.

There are several small scars at the base of my throat. They do not extend very far, and are fainter in color. But lower, over my heart, the skin is puckered and uneven. Dark lines create a grotesque web of flesh that's been there for as long as I can remember.

I clench the scarf tightly as my mind fills with the memory of the first time Mother told me I must wear it. I was very young, and we were still living in England. The weather had been unbearably warm and I wanted to go swimming in the pond with the other children. But when Mother saw me removing the scarf, she pulled me from the water and marched me back to Aunt Isobel's house. The look in her eyes frightened me as she gripped my shoulders. "You must never take off your scarf around anyone else, Annabel! Promise me! Or God will punish you for it."

I was struck with such fear that I have heeded her words ever since.

Turning away from my reflection, I wrap the scarf securely around my neck and pad over to the armoire. There are three new dresses inside—a white one with lace detailing at the neck and sleeves, a pale yellow one with jet-black beading, and a light blue one with a separate jacket. They are all simply stitched, yet beautifully made.

Madame LaFleur may not have wanted to be associated with Father, but she clearly had no qualms over accepting his money.

I choose the blue outfit, and I'm able to dress myself with little trouble. Since I've not yet had a chance to apply the lemon juice and rosewater to my hands to soften them, I pull on the pair of white gloves Madame LaFleur had given me. I slide two silver combs into my hair, and with one final glance in the looking glass, go down to the courtyard.

Cook and Johanna are busy with breakfast preparations, so they take little notice of me as I slip through the kitchen. I'm early for my rendezvous with Allan, and while I wait, my nerves flutter like a thousand butterflies.

Finally, the door from the kitchen opens, and I turn to greet him. "It was many and many a year ago, in a kingdom by the sea," he muses as he looks down at me, "that a maiden there lived whom you may know by the name of Annabel Lee."

He gently kisses my cheek and then takes my hand. "Come with me. I have something I want to read to you."

The sky turns pink and gold around us as we sit on the bench. He reaches inside his pocket and pulls out a folded piece of paper, glancing over at me uncertainly. I give him an encouraging smile.

"I've been working on this recently," he says. "It's a section I am most proud of, though it is still in rough form. Pray do not be too hasty in your criticism."

"I would not dream of it." I smile at him again, and he begins to read.

"When I had waited a long time, very patiently, without hearing him lie down, I resolved to open a little—a very, very little crevice in the lantern. So I opened it—you cannot imagine how stealthily, stealthily—until, at length a simple dim ray, like the thread of the spider, shot from out the crevice and fell full upon the vulture eye.

"It was open—wide, wide open—and I grew furious as I gazed upon it. I saw it with perfect distinctness— all a dull blue, with a hideous veil over it that chilled the very marrow in my bones; but I could see nothing else of the old man's face or person: for I had directed the ray as if by instinct, precisely upon the damned spot.

"And have I not told you that what you mistake for madness is but overacuteness of the sense?—now, I say, there came to my ears a low, dull, quick sound, such as a watch makes when enveloped in cotton. I knew that sound well, too. It was the beating of the old man's heart. It increased my fury, as the beating of a drum stimulates the soldier into courage. . . ."

Allan's words remind me of the crier's news at the market, and suddenly I'm rising to my feet.

"It's very good," I say, with only a slight tremor to my voice.

Allan stands, too. "You liked it?" He reaches for my hand, but I notice his palm is scratched.

"You've hurt yourself."

He glances down. "I had not realized. It must have happened last night."

I look at his hand again. "You were working with my father, weren't you?"

"Of course."

"Were you with him the entire time?"

"He had need of supplies. I went to the apothecary to fetch them."

"And the apothecary was open at such a late hour? Was Mr. Williams there?" I feel my excitement rising. "Perhaps you saw something, or heard something, that might lead to finding his murderer!"

Allan closes his eyes for a moment, and puts out a hand to steady himself.

Alarmed, I touch his cheek. "You look weary. You have been working too much. What could Father possibly need at such a late hour?"

His eyes go blank. "I don't recall."

"Surely, it must have been important."

"Yes. I am certain it was."

"You don't remember?"

Before he can answer, Johanna's voice interrupts us. "Miss! Where are you, miss?"

I hastily pull away from Allan, and moments later, she joins us.

"Breakfast is ready, an' the Grandmaster was asking where you were."

"It seems we must say our good-byes then," Allan says.

I search his eyes for a moment, trying to read the truth in them. But there is only weariness and confusion. I remove my hand and curtsy to him. "Until next time."

Johanna leads the way into the kitchen and I follow, casting a glance at Allan over my shoulder. He watches me leave, but the look on his face is very strange. It's almost as if he's remembering something.

※　※　※

"Your father informed me that your teacher has been dismissed, so you will be free to do as you wish until a replacement can be found," Grand-père announces once we've finished breakfast.

I don't know if I should tell him that I am already aware of the note of dismissal Mrs. Tusk received, so I simply nod. "I understand, Grand-père."

He looks directly at the side of my face, and I glance guiltily down at the floor. *Does he know what Mrs. Tusk did?* My face did not bruise where she struck me, and with no evidence left behind, I thought I didn't need to tell him about it.

"One of the staff informed me of Mrs. Tusk's deplorable behavior." He looks upset. "I'm sorry you had to experience such a thing, Annabel. It will not happen again."

Impulsively, I give him a quick hug and then kiss his cheek. "It's already forgotten. Do not be angered on my behalf, Grand-père."

He pats my back. "I shall endeavor to be as forgiving as you are, my dear. Enjoy your day. I shall see you again at dinner."

"Enjoy your day as well." I give him another kiss and leave the room. On my way up the staircase, though, Maddy comes rushing down. Tears streak her face, and she lifts a corner of her apron to wipe her eyes. I put out a hand to stop her from colliding with me. "What's wrong, Maddy? Have you received more news about your mother?"

"It's my locket, miss. I lost it."

"Where did you last see it?"

"I don't know!" she wails. "Cook sent me to the market this morning, but I didn't find it was gone until just now. I can't remember if I put it back on last night after I hauled yer bath water."

"Have you checked the kitchen?"

She shakes her head. "Cook and Johanna both helped me look fer it, but it's not there." Her eyes start to fill with tears again.

"Why don't we go to the market?" I suggest. "We can retrace your steps from this morning. Let me go fetch my cloak."

Maddy nods and waits for me at the bottom of the stairs as I hurry to my room and then swiftly return. We keep our eyes on the ground in search of the locket as we walk toward the marketplace, but we do not find it. Maddy fights to keep her lip from trembling when we learn that none of the vendors we question have come across the locket either.

"Don't worry, Maddy," I reassure her as we finally turn back. "We will not stop looking until it's found."

When we return home, I decide to check my bedroom to see if it was misplaced there when Maddy was inside. But I pause when my eye falls on the book still sitting on my desk—*The Anatomy of Humane Bodies*.

When I first read it, something in the entry for typhus had bothered me. Now, as I read through the passage again, I understand what it was.

> *The disease of Typhus; more commonly known as jail fever; is capable of afflicting the mind as well as the body. Head pain, delirium, and stupor are noted symptoms as well as nausea, arm and leg pain, body fever, and red sores. These sores can lead to rotting flesh and gangrenous limbs. Believed to be caused by rats, the best prevention is to keep one's home and property as free from vermin as possible. Once the disease has spread, there is no known cure.*

Father's symptoms do not fit the description. He's not plagued by delirium and stupor, but by ill temper.

He does not walk around in a fog or forget who he is. And he does not suffer red sores and rotting flesh. If Father truly does not have typhus, then why did Grand-père purposely mislead me?

Nineteen

I volunteer to search further for Maddy's locket, but when evening comes, I still have not found it. And thoughts of Grand-père's deception weigh heavily on my mind. I go to his study and find him at the desk. "I have something I need to discuss with you, Grand-père. Do you have a moment?"

He looks up. "This sounds quite serious. Is something the matter?"

I take a deep breath to steady my nerves. Am I really about to ask him if he's been deceiving me? "Forgive me for contradicting you, but a passage in one of my medical books describes typhus in great detail, and Father does not seem to have the symptoms. I thought you said that's the disease he suffers from."

Grand-père clears his throat and glances down at the papers in front of him. "It's a complicated matter. One that your father should be discussing with you instead of me."

"But, Grand-père, Father does not have any time for me. He rarely joins us for meals, and even then—"

He holds up one hand to stop me. "I know you've had your frustrations with him, so I will tell you this. . . . Markus was a brilliant doctor. But he was also a brilliant scientist. When he was younger, he tried to combine the two, and the results were not what he expected. He did, indeed, contract typhus while in France, though. The scientific community there did not understand the work he was doing, and he was sentenced to six months of prison labor. That's where he contracted the disease."

Grand-père falls silent. "Your father created a serum that he thought would cure him. Although it helped with some of the minor symptoms of the disease, it did not work entirely. Ever since, it has been his life's work to perfect that serum. But I fear his failures have only made matters worse. Truth be told, my dear, that's why I came to live here with him. I saw how the failures weighed upon him, and I thought I could help."

Grand-père gives me a gentle smile. "Forgive me, I'm sure you were not looking for a history lesson. Was there anything else you wanted to ask me?"

"No, Grand-père. There's nothing more." I curtsy, and then find myself hugging him. "Thank you for telling me the truth about Father. Sleep well."

He returns my hug. "Ahem. Yes. Well, then, sleep well."

❦   ❦   ❦

Eventually, I succumb to sleep, though my head is full of dark dreams, and when the clock outside my door chimes three, I'm suddenly awakened.

I lie still, trying to determine what has woken me. Something tells me that the answers lie downstairs in Father's laboratory.

My dressing gown floats around my feet as I move silently through the house. A full moon lights my path. The kitchen is empty when I finally enter, while the door to the laboratory stands open. The key still hangs in the lock. Gathering my courage, I take a step, and go through the door.

The air in the stairwell is increasingly cold, and a familiar scent teases the edges of my memories. When I reach the bottom, I find the door there is open as well. I creep silently closer.

The operating theater is dark—only a single candle burns on the table—and I slowly enter. The smell is stronger inside the room, acidic and tangy, and my mind races as I try to place it. I feel my eyes widen when recognition finally comes.

Blood.

I blindly step back and bump into something. Reaching behind me, my fingers encounter two large wheels and a handle connected to them, then the seat of a chair. It's some sort of wheeled contraption.

A faint shuffling sound comes from outside the room, and I freeze. Someone is coming down the stairs.

My heart speeds up. *Father. He's coming this way.*

I scramble to hide behind the wheeled chair and try desperately to slow my shallow breathing. Something frantic pulses at the base of my neck, and I pray that the darkness will hide me. I do not want to be found like this.

A figure enters the room and walks slowly toward the table. He drags a burlap sack, and with a grunt, he hauls it up onto the table.

A lifeless arm suddenly flops out of the sack.

I bite down hard on my thumb so I don't scream.

I don't know what to do. I cannot be discovered! Father has already shown how angry he becomes when I displease him. If he were to find out what I've witnessed, who knows what he might do?

Something rolls off the table and he curses. His back is turned to me as he bends to retrieve the object, and I know I must make my escape.

I slowly stand. But just as I take my first step, he holds up the retrieved item.

It's a cane.

I gasp, and he turns around instantly. "Who's there?"

The voice is not my Father's. It's Edgar's.

I stumble against the wheeled chair. Flinging out a hand to catch myself, I feel glass beneath my fingers only moments before a jar crashes to the ground. The sound ricochets around me.

"Stop!" Edgar shouts.

I knock more jars off the shelves, trying frantically to regain my footing. A sharp *pop, pop, pop* comes, one right after another. The room is closing in on me. It's too hard to breathe.

I see myself being trapped in this room forever with Edgar as he slowly murders me and leaves my body to rot. I whimper at the thought. My panic is turning me into a caged animal and I blindly pull things off the shelf in a desperate attempt to break free.

I don't hear him come up behind me, but he grabs my arm. I thrash wildly, until he reaches for my other arm and pins them at my sides. "Annabel?" he says.

"Please," I gasp. Tears are choking me, and I cannot draw a breath. "Let me go. Please . . . I beg of you."

He pulls me closer to still my body, and the gesture makes me think of how only hours ago I was embracing Allan. Wanting nothing to taint that memory, I say, "I will not scream. But you must let me go. I cannot breathe."

He pauses a moment, then releases me. I draw in a deep breath as I try to gain control of my thoughts.

"How long have you been here?" he demands.

"Only a short time. I thought my father was down here."

He glances over at the body on the table. "He was."

Tears instantly fill my eyes. "Is that . . . is that . . ." I cannot say the words.

"You mean is that him?" Edgar glances back at me. "It's not, if that's what you were thinking."

Relief floods through me.

"He *was* here, but he left me to take care of this." Edgar waves carelessly at the body, as if it's nothing more than a place setting. "He is the doctor, and I am the student after all. A student's work can be quite . . . messy at times."

I stare at him. "I don't understand what you mean."

"He commits the act, and I clean up after him. It's rather simple."

"Are you saying my father is a murderer?"

"Bird, flying because it's supposed to fly? Remember? We had this conversation already. Now"—he grabs my elbow—"if you will be so kind as to come with me. I have a long night of disposal ahead of me, and I should like to get back to it."

He marches me toward the door. "Naturally, you cannot speak of this to anyone. Your father would be arrested for his crimes. Almost *certainly* hanged. Shame would come upon your family name, the house would be sold, the fortune lost. . . . And, as far as the deceased, well, I don't think anyone will be missing her."

I keep my eyes cast down as we walk—I do not wish

to see what they have done—but as we draw closer to the table, my eyes betray me. My feet come to a sudden stop. The edges of the sack are open, exposing the lifeless body lying on the table.

It's Mrs. Tusk.

Twenty

Edgar forces me up to my bedroom, holding on to my arm the entire way. As soon as he lets go of me, I whirl around to face him. But the door shuts just as quickly as it was opened, and I hear the unmistakable sound of a key turning in the lock. I pound on the door, but his footsteps have already started to fade. "No!" I cry. "Let me out! Let me out!"

He does not return, and after several minutes of futile banging, I realize no one can hear me.

I move to the window. *Perhaps I can climb down.* But I quickly see I'm too high up. The outside wall is smooth, and offers no chance of escape. Frustrated, I clench my hands. *I must tell someone what Edgar's done!*

My throat begins to tighten, and I cough several times. Then my eyes start to burn. The air is growing heavier. Almost as if a window has been opened, and a thick fog is creeping in.

And then I realize, it isn't fog inside my bedroom—it's smoke.

Hurrying to the door, I bang again and again. I glance around wildly, desperate for something that can break through the solid wood. My gaze falls on the bedside table and I move to pick it up, when I see something else. Something better. The button Maddy told me to use to get her attention.

I push the button until I hear feet running down the hallway. The doorknob rattles when someone tries to open it from the other side.

"Miss Annabel!" Maddy yells. "Annabel! Yer door is locked. Do you know what happened to the key? The house is on fire! We must get out!"

I put my face up close to the door. The smoke makes my eyes water. "It was taken. Can you get the keys from Cook?"

Silence greets me.

"Maddy?" I bang on the door again. "Maddy!"

A sound comes from the knob below my hand, and I glance down. It is a key being fitted into the lock. The door swings open, and I see Maddy there, chest heaving, eyes wide. She holds a damp cloth to her face, covering her nose. "I remembered the skeleton was at the end of the hall, Miss Annabel!" she says triumphantly.

"Good girl, Maddy." I grab her hand and pull her toward the staircase leading to the kitchen. I can hear footsteps running through the house and someone yelling below, only now I can make out the words being shouted. "*Fire! Fire!*"

Maddy pulls back on my hand, forcing me to stop. "Not that way! The fire started down there. We have to use the main stairs."

Reversing our course, we hurry down as fast as we can. When we reach the great room, Cook comes rushing toward us. Her arms are filled with silver platters. "Miss!" she says urgently. "Come with me!"

"Where's Grand-père? Is he still in his study?"

She shakes her head. "He's fine, miss. He was the first one to alert us to the fire. Come now, we've got to get you out. I tried to save what I could—"

"What about Father?"

Maddy tugs on my hand again and urges me to the door. "The Master is probably outside, Miss Annabel."

"Where was he the last time you saw him?" She looks down at the ground and quickly shakes her head. "Cook?" I demand. "Do you know where my father is?"

"I think he was in the laboratory, miss. But you can't—"

I push Maddy toward her. "Go! Go! I won't leave without Father. I must find him!"

Maddy tries one last time to make me come with her, but I slip free from her grasp. "At least take this with you, Miss Annabel," she says, handing me the wet cloth.

I take it from her and turn in the direction of the dining room. The walls are black, and I cannot stop coughing even though I'm breathing through the cloth.

My vision only seems to get worse as I keep moving. Stumbling into the kitchen, I narrowly miss stepping on a hutch that's fallen over. Broken dishes cover the floor. Even though there are no flames, the smoke is overwhelming. I call for Father until my throat grows weak, and I make my way over to the door that leads down to the laboratory.

The knob is hot to the touch, and I don't realize my fingers are burned until it's too late. I pull back, but my skin is already red and blistered. Using the sleeve of my dressing gown as a buffer, I turn the knob again. When the door opens, smoke billows out.

I drop to my knees. The fire must have started in the laboratory.

"Father!" I cry weakly. "Father!" But I can no longer tell if any sound is coming out. My throat seizes up as a coughing fit overcomes me. "Father . . ."

His name is a whisper.

Suddenly, someone grabs my shoulder and pulls me back from the door. Then I'm lifted into the air.

"Annabel!" a voice yells into my ear. My rescuer stumbles and curses. His voice is faint, but it sounds like Allan. Catching himself, he carries me across the kitchen. He stumbles again and I almost fall from his arms. "Damn you!" he yells down at me.

I struggle to lift my head. *Why is he so upset with me?*

He stumbles once more, and then, finally, we are free. The air outside is a soothing balm to my lungs, and he lays me on the ground.

"What were you doing down there?" he asks.

I try to speak, but can't. Coughing again, I rub my

soot-filled eyes and look up at him. Allan's hair has come loose and the collar of his shirt is ripped.

"*Why were you down there?*" he says angrily.

My vision is still blurry, but his face starts to become clearer.

"Edgar?" I say hoarsely.

He pulls back abruptly. Without another word, he crosses the courtyard and then disappears through the gate that leads to the cobblestone street beyond.

❋   ❋   ❋

I lie on the ground, drinking in the cold night air as my chest heaves, and I lose all sense of time. My hearing is muffled, but I recognize voices in the distance. "Cook! Johanna!" I call weakly. "I'm here!"

The gate opens and Johanna comes charging through it. "Miss!" she yells. She turns her head and shouts over her shoulder, "Back here! She's back here!"

Cook immediately rushes in behind her, and when they reach me, they each put an arm around me. "Has Father been found?" I ask. "Has everyone made it out of the house?"

"All's fine," Cook says soothingly. "Maddy is with the Grandmaster, an' the Master is directing Jasper an' Thomas to put the fire out."

Helping me to my feet, they lead me around to the front of the house. I breathe a sigh of relief when I see Grand-père's white hair.

"Grand-père!" I shout his name and pull away from Cook and Johanna. My legs are weak, but I run toward him. Tears stream down my face.

He gathers me close. "Shhhh, shhhh," he says. "You are safe."

"I could not find Father. . . . I thought he was trapped in his laboratory."

Grand-père points to the left. "Your father is safe. See? He's overseeing the water brigade."

I look to where Grand-père points. Father is limping toward the far side of the house, directing Thomas and Jasper, who carry buckets of water into the house through an open window. Cook and Johanna come to stand beside me. A small pile of silver rests at Cook's feet. Maddy joins me, and we share a brief hug.

"I'm so glad yer safe, miss," she says. "You gave me a scare."

"I'm fine now, Maddy. Thanks to your quick think-ing." She nods, and I turn to Grand-père. "What happened? How did the fire start?"

He shakes his head. "We cannot be sure. I'm just thankful that everyone is safe."

Smoke billows out of a nearby window, and a black cloud of ash rises above us. "But what about the house?" I ask. "What about everything that will be lost?"

Grand-père waves his hand. "Although there's a lot of smoke, the flames have not reached very far. Besides, things can be replaced. People cannot." He looks down at me. "I'm so thankful you are safe, Annabel. I—"

A grimace crosses his face, and he clutches his chest. "I—"

He suddenly falls backward.

"Grand-père!" I scream. I bend down beside him and reach for his hand. "Grand-père, what's wrong?"

His eyes are open, but they do not blink. His face still bears a grimace.

"Grand-père?" I whimper. I squeeze his fingers. There is no response. I put a hand on his chest to see the steady rise and fall, but it does not rise. "Grand-père!" I scream again. "Grand-père, no!"

Leaning over, I pat his face. "Grand-père! Grand-père! Wake up, Grand-père. You must wake up!" But he does not respond.

Maddy tries to get my attention. "Annabel. Miss. He—"

"Father!" I scream, getting to my feet. "Father, it's Grand-père! Come quickly!" I can barely see for the tears filling my eyes. But I make my way to Father's side.

Alarm fills his face. "Annabel, what . . . ?"

I shake my head as the words come tumbling out of me. "Grand-père's chest is not rising. He's stopped breathing. You must come now, Father. Come help him."

Father hurries to Grand-père's side as fast as his stilted gait will allow. Bending down, he puts his ear close to Grand-père's mouth and listens for breath. Father's face grows paler. He starts to pound on Grand-père's chest, and after each motion, pauses to listen again.

When he finally looks up at me, his eyes are blank. "He's dead."

I shake my head. Father gets to his feet and takes a step toward me, but I keep shaking my head. "It cannot be true. I know you're a doctor. You must do something. *Do something!*" I hear the words rising as I say it again and again. "It cannot be true! It cannot be true!

Do something, Father. Help him!"

The world suddenly comes to a stop. All I can hear is the anguish in my own voice. And that anguish is the last thing I remember.

Twenty-One

I come to when a patch of afternoon sunlight slants across my face. Sitting up, I take in everything around me. I'm safe in my own bed. Not outside watching smoke pour out of my new home. Not clutching the lifeless fingers of Grand-père. Not being carried from the depths of a smoky hell by Allan . . . or Edgar.

My heart lifts—*it must have been a dream.*

I throw aside the covers, then instantly pull back my hand as pain races through my fingers. I look down at them. They're red and blistered.

It was not a dream after all.

Shock turns to numbness as I stare down at my hands. My chest constricts, like I'm being laced into a corset that is drawn tighter and tighter and my every breath hurts. I wait for the pain to go away, but it clings to me like a second skin, and even as I rise from the bed, I cannot shake the feeling.

Stopping in front of the looking glass, I search my face for signs of grief. Of pain. Surely, my eyes should be filled with tears and my heart aching from the loss of Grand-père. But there is nothing. Nothing but this tightness that wraps around my chest and constricts my lungs, becoming one with me, matching every breath I take and every move I make. This *thing* has slipped beneath my skin like a second person. This *thing* is the reason why I do not cry. Why I go through the motions of dressing myself in a simple gown. Why I pull on neat white gloves over aching fingers with barely a whimper. This *thing* propels me to go downstairs even though I should rage and yell and ask the heavens why Grand-père would be taken from me like this. Why the only person to truly understand me in this house could be gone in the blink of an eye. It makes me act as though I do not care. It's why I am unfeeling.

True horror washes over me then. And I realize, I'm just like my father. Coldness and callousness are my birthright. They are in my blood.

I wander downstairs in a haze of disbelief and find myself in the great room. The scent of smoke still lingers in the air. Outside the dining room doors, Cook has set up tables with platters of food piled upon them. I pour myself a cup of tea and take it to the courtyard.

The larder appears to have sustained the most damage in the kitchen—everything is burned and covered in ash—while in the corner near the door that leads to Father's laboratory, a beam from the ceiling has partially fallen. The courtyard door is standing open to let in fresh air, and I have to step carefully as I make my way over to it.

Once I'm outside, I sit down on the bench where Maddy and I had our picnic and stare down into my tea. My mind is impossibly full, yet impossibly blank. *How can I be so cold? So unfeeling? Why can I not grieve for Grand-père?*

I hear the sound of a cane tapping on the ground, but I don't look up. Edgar saunters over and takes a seat beside me. "Rough time of it last night?"

I stay silent.

"I must say, I was rather hoping for a thank-you."

"A *thank-you?*" I am in no mood to be dealing with him right now.

"I saved your life."

Fury boils inside of me. "You're the reason why I was trapped during the fire! How dare you lock me in like that!"

He sighs dramatically. "You interrupted my work. What choice did I have?" He glances down at his nails and begins to pick at one of them. "Besides, I carried you out, didn't I? I could have just left you down there to burn."

My fury goes cold. "Perhaps you should have."

"Pardon?" He leans toward me. "I could not quite hear that."

"I *said*, perhaps you should have left me there."

"Poor, poor Annabel." His voice is mocking. "Was your sleep interrupted by the fire? Did you have bad dreams?"

My own voice is as sharp as glass. I barely recognize it. "Grand-père died last night. His heart stopped from the excitement."

Edgar waves a hand dismissively. "It was his time, then. He *was* rather old. . . ."

Anger boils in my blood again, red-hot, and the sharp crack of my hand against his cheek echoes around us. "How can you say such a thing?" I seethe.

Edgar looks momentarily stunned. Then his expression turns to amusement. "Bravo. I didn't know you had it in you." He gives me a polite clap and smiles broadly. "Felt good, didn't it?"

I ignore his baiting tone. "Grand-père was honest and trustworthy and loyal. He should have lived a long life. Much longer than he was allowed."

"Are you implying that I am none of those things?"

"*You* are a murderer."

"Not true." He taps his cane against the side of the bench. "Your father is the murderer. I am merely his assistant."

Edgar's verbal parrying frustrates me, and I have no further desire to be in his company. Turning away from him, I stare at the horizon. The sun is sinking and night will soon start to fall. "Why are you here, Edgar?" I say abruptly. "What do you want?"

"The weather is growing colder, and you have something that belongs to me. I need it returned."

I turn to face him again. "Something of *yours*? I have nothing of yours."

Edgar taps his shoulder with his cane. "My coat? I was most gentlemanly and lent it to you."

He's right. I do have his coat. The morning I helped Maddy's mother, I dropped it in the back of the armoire as soon as I returned to my room so I would not have to see it and be reminded of what happened. Now I find myself wishing it had burned in the fire. "Wait here," I say stiffly, leaving my cup of tea behind. "I'll retrieve it for you."

I find Edgar's coat on the floor of the armoire, just as I remembered. Shaking my head, I gingerly pick up the crumpled piece of clothing. But the sound of crinkling paper stops me.

Carrying the jacket over to the window, I look inside the pocket and find a small slip of paper. There are several lines written on it.

The Heart That Told No Tales

The Tale; A Heart That Tells

Telling the Tale of a Morbid Heart

The Tell-Tale Heart

The last line is circled. I turn the paper over and find more scribbles there in a heavy hand.

WHERE IS THE HEART???

CUPBOARD? CLOSET?

And then just a single word:

FLOORBOARDS.

I drop the paper like it just singed my fingertips. *Mr. Williams's heart was missing, and it was later found beneath the floorboards. . . .*

Edgar had been planning that murder. He is the one responsible.

I go to the bed and remove Mother's book from beneath my pillow, stroking the worn cover as I think about what to do. It repulses me to have to touch that piece of paper again. But if I don't put it inside the coat, Edgar will know I have found it.

With a grimace, I pick the paper up from the floor and carefully place it deep inside the pocket. Edgar sits waiting with an impatient expression on his face when I return, and I toss the coat toward him. "There you are."

He catches it neatly and stands. "You know, you have further need to thank me."

"You shall have a very long wait, then, because I see no reason to thank you for anything." I'm so upset that I forget I'm still clutching the zodiac book.

"Even though I have spared your father?"

His words give me pause. "Spared my father from what?"

"From being hanged as a murderer."

"How have you done that?"

"It was rather simple. Your maid . . . Maddy . . . is it? She was the answer. When Mrs. Tusk's body is found, she'll be clutching a locket. A locket that belongs to the person who murdered her."

He cannot mean . . . "You intend to place Maddy's locket on Mrs. Tusk's corpse?"

Edgar tips his head at me. "Do you not think it brilliant?"

"How did you even come upon it?"

"I found it in the kitchen. She should be more careful where she sets her things. But then"—he shrugs disdainfully—"what do you expect from the help?"

"I will tell everyone the truth." A blinding rage so fierce I have never felt the like comes over me, and my hands start to tremble. "I will tell them that you are the murderer. That I saw you standing over Mrs. Tusk's lifeless body." I grip Mother's book tightly so I don't throw it at him.

"I know what you did to Mr. Williams, as well. I have found your thoughts on murder," I hiss. "In the pocket of your overcoat."

"Not just me." Edgar wags his finger. "You shall

have to tell everyone what your *father* and I have done to poor Mr. Williams."

My stomach lurches. I'm going to be sick. "How could you?" I stare at him, and he grins delightedly.

"It was just another name on a long list, my dear. Williams was well acquainted with Mrs. Tusk, it seems, and they wanted to blackmail your father for money."

The apothecary shop Mr. Williams was the same Mr. Williams I overheard Mrs. Tusk talking to Father about? Can it be true? Did he really have something to do with their deaths?

I am horrified by my thoughts.

The slip of paper with those horrible words written on it falls from Edgar's coat pocket, and he stoops to retrieve it. He stares down at it in reverence. "These are not merely thoughts on murder. They are the beginning of a story."

"A story? You are recording your horrors?"

"How am I to accurately write about something unless I've been a firsthand witness to it?"

I tear the paper from his hand and crumple it in my fist. "Have you no shame? These words are disgusting."

He looks amused. "I wonder if you would think that if someone else had written them? Perhaps Allan—"

"Allan would never write such filth!"

"Wouldn't he?" Edgar slowly reaches into his pocket and withdraws a small glass vial filled with brown liquid. Right before he uncorks it and puts it to his lips, he says, "Let's find out, shall we?"

Twenty-Two

A s soon as Edgar drinks the liquid, he starts to convulse. His body shakes so fiercely that I fear the vial will be crushed within his clenched fist. He throws his head back, and his jaw snaps shut. Deep moans rattle from between his teeth.

The sounds are horrible. It is like listening to a dying animal.

His head bows, and the bones in his shoulders creak. A ripple runs beneath his shirt and he slowly stands up straight. The convulsing continues and then he lifts his head.

The hint of a beard is no longer there, and the lines that were once etched deeply upon his face begin to fade away. His eyes soften, changing from small pinpoints of darkness to a deep brown that I've seen before.

The shaking stops. He blinks. And I realize it's no longer Edgar standing before me.

It's Allan.

"What's happening?" Allan's face is filled with confusion. "Annabel? How did I get here? I was just—"

My mind cannot comprehend what I've just witnessed.

"How did I get here?" he says hoarsely.

"I . . . I don't know." I'm as confused as he is. How can this be? Where did Edgar go? How did Allan come to be standing in his place?

"What happened?" He takes a step toward me, and without thinking, I draw back. Surprise comes over his face, and then it turns to horror. "Dear God . . ." He looks down at his hands. "What have I done? Annabel, please, you must tell me. What have I *done*?"

"N-nothing." I take another step back, but then chide myself for doing so. *This is Allan. I'm not afraid of him.* "Do you remember anything? Edgar was here only moments ago and then he—"

"Edgar? How do you know that name? I don't like to use it. It brings back unpleasant memories."

Understanding dawns on me. "*Your* name is Edgar?"

"My proper name is Edgar Allan Poe. The only person who knows me as such is your father."

I put a hand to my cheek. I'm burning up. I must be overly tired and delirious from the excitement of the fire last night. There is no other explanation for what has just transpired. Glancing down, I see the crumpled paper in my hand. "Have you ever seen this before?" I hold the paper out to him and he slowly takes it from me.

Smoothing the creases, he's silent as he reads. Finally, he says, "Where did you get this?"

"From Edgar's coat."

Edgar's overcoat is still lying at Allan's feet and he bends to pick it up. His brow furrows. "You said this was in *his* coat?"

I nod.

"But this is *my* coat. . . ." He shifts his attention back to the paper. "Have you read what's written here?"

I nod again, hesitantly. "Several days ago, I met someone in the library who said he was my father's second assistant. And that he was your cousin, Edgar.

We have met several times, and just now . . . moments ago . . . he was here. He was taunting me, asking what I would think if *you* were the one who had written the words on that paper."

"And what would you think of me if I were to write such things, Annabel?"

Before I can answer, he turns away. "You would think me monstrous." He grips his head. "I think it of myself. Why should I want to write of death? But in my darkest moments, I find that I am drawn to the macabre. To the underbelly of things we do not understand. Only when I lose myself can I write so freely, and the feeling is terrifying. To have no control, no remorse, no remembrance of events . . ."

He turns back to face me. "This is the truth of it: These *are* my words, Annabel. My darkest vice. My most dangerous secret. I am him, and he is me. I've never seen Edgar, but I know he's there. I have no control over this. Over . . . *him*. But whatever he is, he gives life to my words. Edgar is the worst of me, and the best of me. Without him, I am nothing."

"I don't understand. How can you be—"

Allan's hands start to tremble. He clenches his teeth and his fingers curl inward. "I can't stop it," he mumbles. "I haven't taken enough."

"Enough of what?"

"Tapping, at my chamber door. I cannot stop this tapping. I must . . ."

A deep moan cuts off his word. I reach for his hand. "Allan?"

He pulls away from me, convulsing violently. Shoulders hunching, back bowing, he lets out another inhuman groan and clenches his fists so tightly I can hear his very bones creaking. When he looks up again, his eyes are hard. His jaw shadowed. Deep lines mark his face, and I know that somehow, *some way*, it's now Edgar standing before me.

Edgar reaches for the cane at his feet and twirls it once before affecting a casual stance. Smoothing back the hair that hangs in his face, he watches me shrewdly. "I expected more from you, Annabel. You are not surprised? Terrified? Repulsed by his weakness?"

"I . . ." My thoughts tumble so quickly over one another that I cannot keep them straight. Visions of Maddy's mother fill my head. *Is Allan like her? Is he mad?*

"You have no interest in how we became this way?"

I try to put the pieces of this puzzle together. "I

have heard of morbid changes in the brain that cause certain . . . afflictions," I say slowly.

"An *affliction*? Is that what you think I am?" He laughs. "I am not his *affliction*. Although it was your father who ultimately released me, I guess you could say I've always been there, just below the surface."

Edgar smirks. "Do you know that your dear Allan is quite mad? I've seen what's inside." He taps the side of his head. "All the bits and bobs that make him *tick*."

With every word, he moves closer.

"He is nothing without me," Edgar continues. "We are two halves of the same whole. Like the conjoined heart in the laboratory. But now I'm the only part worth saving, and it's time to burn the chaff."

Edgar moves swiftly then, grabbing my arm so hard I fear it will bruise. "I will not be controlled like this anymore. You will do as I say, or the next time I set fire to this place, it won't be just your father's laboratory. I shall start with your bedroom."

"*You* started the fire?" My voice is barely a whisper.

"Your father made me very angry. He refused to do as I asked. So I took away the one thing that meant the most to him—his laboratory. Of course, the fire was supposed to have taken care of Mrs. Tusk's body, as well. Pity it didn't burn entirely. Now she will be found clutching her murderer's locket."

Edgar started the fire. . . . And Grand-père was the one to pay the price. Tightness wraps around me again, gripping my insides. "What did you want Father to do?" I finally manage.

"I want him to set me free. So I no longer rely on this cursed serum whenever I wish to come forth." He holds up the empty vial from which he drank and smashes it on the ground. "Allan takes it after your father's experimentations on him, to keep me away, but I want a cure so that when he drinks from it the next time, *I* am the one who stays."

Edgar waits for me to respond, but I have no words. He is mad. Truly mad.

"Swear that you will convince your father to find a way to free me. His fingers dig harshly into my arm, and I cry out. "Swear it."

"He will not listen to me," I say feebly.

"Your precious maid will be next, then. Only I will not burn her. I have been pondering a story in which the character is buried while still alive. I shall need to witness that."

"No!" I pull my arm free from his grasp. "I'll talk to

Father. I swear it! I will find a way."

"Excellent." He twists his cane top and gives me a short bow. "I'm glad we could come to this arrangement."

Twenty-Three

I return to the house as soon as Edgar leaves so I'm not wasting any time in speaking with Father. But my breath catches when I pass Grand-père's study doors. I stop before them.

A soft sound comes from behind me, and I turn around nervously, expecting to see Edgar. But it's only Maddy. Her nose is red and traces of tears stain her cheeks. She sobs, and then covers her mouth with the back of her hand. "I'm sorry, Miss Annabel," she says. "It's so hard to believe. . . ."

"I know, Maddy." I bow my head. I cannot look at her grief.

"His body is inside there." She gestures toward the study. "Mourning customs dictate a laying-in time, but with the fire an' all, I don't know what will happen now." She starts to softly cry again.

"What's wrong with me, Maddy?" I ask desperately. "I cannot cry. Even though I only knew him for a short time, I loved Grand-père as much as I loved my mother. I was able to cry for her. Even to this day, I still cry. But for Grand-père, I can do nothing. . . ."

"Everyone is diff'rent, Miss Annabel. Johanna cried up a great storm, while Cook set to making food. Even now with the kitchen all burned up, she's still cooking. Johanna said it's just her way."

"I don't have a way," I say bitterly. "I'm like Father. Cold and callous."

"That's not true." Maddy gently touches my arm. "I know that's not true." She pulls out the handkerchief I gave her and holds it out to me. "I saw yer caring in this. An' when you brought me yer special tea, an' helped Mama, an' fixed Johanna's finger. You are nothing like yer father, Miss Annabel."

"But all I have is this tightness inside me, Maddy. It wraps around my chest and constricts my lungs. It squeezes the very breath out of me. It's a coldness. Like . . . *him*."

"That's not coldness." Her voice lifts, and I meet her eyes. "Don't you see? It's sorrow. I felt much the same when I learned Mama would never be right. That she would always need someone to watch her. Sorrow slips beneath yer very bones an' wraps you in an embrace that never leaves." She pats my hand. "Even if you can't cry now, one day, you will. You'll find yer way."

Maddy's words sink into me, and my thoughts finally become clear. Suddenly remembering the reason why I returned to the house, Edgar's threat, I grip her fingers. "Have you seen my father? I must speak with him. It's urgent."

"He left early this morning, right after the fire. Said he was meeting someone an' would be gone all day."

I touch my scarf. "Please let me know the moment he returns, Maddy. I have need to speak with him right away."

She nods and I turn toward the stairs, silently urging Father to hurry back home. Until he returns, all I can do is hope Edgar doesn't grow too impatient. For now, we both must wait.

🦋 🦋 🦋

As the hour grows late, I cannot sleep. Father has not yet returned, and I'm pacing the confines of my room. When I hear a knock at the door, I open it to find Johanna holding a letter.

"This came for you, miss." She offers it to me with a slight bob of her head. Her expression is one of curiosity. "It was delivered by Master Allan."

It's very strange for me to receive a letter at such a late hour. But this has been a strange day. Thanking her, I wait until she's gone before I open it. The dark script says:

> I MUST SEE YOU —
> 12TH AND PINE STREETS
> # 4
> A.

My heart beats fast at the thought of going to him. Hurrying to the armoire, I remove my cloak and put it on. I place the letter in the pocket and find Johanna again to ask for directions. It's not far, only two streets over, and she tells me to follow the cobbled alleyway.

Slipping out the kitchen door, I cross the courtyard under the light of a half-moon. It takes me little time to find where 12th and Pine streets intersect. There's a house on the corner, with a sign on the door that says rooms are available. A bust of Pallas Athena greets me as I step inside, and a long hallway stretches out before me. Room number four is the second door on the left.

I knock quietly and pray that Allan answers quickly. *If anyone sees me . . .* But there is no answer, and when I knock again, the door gives beneath my fingertips. Silently, I enter.

My breath is quick. It abandons me, then rushes back so fiercely I fear I'm going to faint. The horrors— such horrors!—lie before me.

Blood is everywhere. Splashed on the walls and spilled across the floor. The scent, heavy upon the air, is like a fog that rises up early in the morning. Loops of glistening flesh are strung out upon a table, and in the middle of it all is a single lock of hair. Dark. Curled. Obscene in its loveliness amongst such carnage. I cannot comprehend that such a horrible act has been committed upon someone, and I close my eyes to say a silent prayer for their soul.

I've been witness to grim scenes as Mother's assistant, but nothing could prepare me for this. Only moments ago, this poor person was alive. And now . . .

A sound comes from behind me. I whirl around, and Edgar steps out of the shadows. "Do you like it?"

he purrs. "The small intestine stretches quite far. It is remarkable."

"You did this?"

At his nod, I put one hand up to cover my mouth. Bile rises in the back of my throat and nausea threatens to overcome me. "Why . . . ?"

"To show you that I keep my word. If you deny my request, this will be Cook next. Carved upon my table like a Christmas ham. Or perhaps Johanna."

I take a step back and stumble. "I tried to find Father . . . to speak with him . . . But he's gone out of town and has not yet returned."

Voices come from outside the room, and Edgar springs into action, pushing the door shut behind me, and shoving me backward. Curling his fingers into the collar of my cloak, he holds me up against the wall. My feet barely brush the floor.

"It's my best work yet," Edgar says. "Although rather messy." His voice, low in my ear, is taunting. "Don't you think?"

My heart thumps, and I silently beg him to let me go. To erase this horror from my mad, feverish brain. To let this torment finally come to an end.

His leg is pressed against mine and I feel the heat

of his body singeing me through my dress. He pulls back to study me, cocking his head to one side, and I do what I should have done from the moment he first laid his hands on me—I struggle.

But Edgar holds me tight. He dips his head, and his mouth is dangerously close to my throat. He pushes aside my scarf and I cry out.

And then, suddenly, he lets me go.

Blindly, I stumble away from him. With one hand against the wall, I feel my way toward the door. If I can only be free of this room, away from this house, I know I will be safe.

"Annabel," he calls out, and something in his voice gives me pause. "Do not forget your promise."

Twenty-Four

I keep one hand on my mouth as I find my way back to Father's house. The horrors of that room will not leave my mind. It wasn't Allan who wanted to meet me, it was Edgar. He drew me to that place so I could see what he's capable of.

I rush upstairs to my room. Reaching for Mother's book, I trace the indentation of words on the worn front cover. I don't know what to do. With Grandpère gone, I have no one to confide in. I tuck the book inside my bodice, keeping it close to my heart.

A knock on the door startles me, and then Maddy

says, "Are you still awake, Miss Annabel? Yer father has returned."

"Thank you, Maddy," I call out. "I'll be down in a moment."

A sharp rattling against the window punctuates my words as raindrops start to fall hard and fast. The wind gusts against the panes of glass and the unmistakable sound of thunder echoes ominously. It seems a fierce storm has followed Father home.

The rain is so loud it sounds like troops of soldiers on the march. With lightning streaking the sky, and thunder echoing all around me, I nervously fidget with my scarf.

Finally telling myself that I can wait no longer, I go down to the kitchen. The door to the laboratory is open, and I hear sounds of someone cursing faintly down below. Steeling myself, I touch Mother's book again for strength. I don't want to go down there. Especially with the storm. But I *must* speak with Father. Edgar needs to be stopped.

Black smoke stains cover the walls, and the air becomes heavier as I descend. I stop outside the door that leads to Father's operating theater. *You must go in,* I tell myself.

When I finally enter the room, the damage is devastating. Parts of the ceiling have collapsed, the table is cracked in two, and broken glass covers the floor. What remains of the surgical instruments are melted lumps of silver. I draw in a sharp breath.

Father's voice surprises me. "Annabel, what are you doing down here?" He's standing near a damaged wall on my left, amid a pile of debris. Where I expect to see anger, I see only sadness. "It's not safe."

"I need to speak with you."

He steps toward me, but his eyes are glazed over. As though he's seeing something from another time and place. "You look so much like your mother," he says suddenly. "Do you know that?"

A flash of lightning fills the room and makes me glance nervously toward the narrow windows and touch my scarf.

"She was the only one who truly understood me," he says, almost dreamily. "Or at least, I thought she did. Did you know she helped me perform my surgeries?" He chuckles. "No. Of course you would not know that."

Another flash of lightning comes, followed by thunder so loud it makes me clench my fists with terror.

Father looks to the windows and then back to me. "Are you frightened of storms?"

I nod.

"How long have you felt this fear?"

"For as long as I can remember."

Another crash of thunder sounds, and it feels as if the very house is being shaken. My panic rises. The room feels like it's closing in. "I need to speak to you about Edgar, Father," I say urgently. "We are in danger. I saw him standing over the body of Mrs. Tusk last night, and he was the one who set the fire."

Father scowls. "He was responsible for the fire?"

"Yes. He came to me in the garden and told me I have to persuade you to find a way to make him stay. To rid him of Allan forever. He is mad, Father. He said something about a serum. The next time Allan drinks it, Edgar wants to be the only one who remains." I reach for Father's arm. "I know what you've done."

"What *I* have done?" Father asks in surprise. "You say Edgar was standing over the body of Mrs. Tusk. Has he harmed her?"

"She's dead, Father. He said you are the teacher, and he is the student. I thought you were helping him. But now . . ."—I close my eyes, remembering the awful thing Edgar has shown me—"now he's taken to murdering on his own."

"How could you think I would have anything to do with taking a life?" Father sounds genuinely confused.

"I overheard your conversation with Mrs. Tusk. She said she and Mr. Williams were waiting. She threatened to expose you. Edgar told me they were blackmailing you, and I thought . . ." I glance away.

"You thought I told Edgar to *murder them?*" He looks baffled. "Williams knew of some illegal deliveries I'd made, and he told Mrs. Tusk about them. Although I'm still rather upset by the notion that they were trying to blackmail me, I would not *kill* either one of them because of it."

"What of the day we were having tea, and I told you I heard of Mr. Durham's death? You said that was to be his comeuppance."

Father waves his hand. "Thoughtless words said in anger. Nothing more. Durham once stole some notes from my library."

"What were you having delivered, Father?" I think back to the two men carrying burlap bags. "I have witnessed these deliveries as well."

He clears his throat. "When necessary, I employ

people of a . . . certain nature to bring me cadavers for my work. There has never been a need for me to kill someone for such purposes. I'm interested in preserving human life. Not taking it."

"And the serum? What's in it? What did you create?"

"I thought it would be a cure for typhus. That if I approached it as a disease of the brain, and created a compound to treat it as such, I might have success. I hired Allan to assist me on the project so I could have a controlled subject."

"But he doesn't have typhus. Did you give him the serum *knowing* he did not have the disease?"

"I had to know the effects on a healthy subject."

I'm horrified by his words. "Allan is not a *subject*, Father."

"I'm not proud of my actions, Annabel, but it was necessary." He picks up a glass bottle from the shelf beside him that's been spared from the fire. Wiping away the soot, he peers at the brown liquid inside. "The experiment was not a success, and I quickly noticed the serum was flawed. It brought out a different side of Allan—a darker side. I began to study him, and soon realized he was behaving as if he had two distinct personalities. One was the upright, moral Allan, while the other refused to be recognized by that name. He was Edgar—the embodiment of all of mankind's darkest urges and flawed emotions. When he was Allan, he could not recall what Edgar had done. And when he was Edgar, he could not recall how he acted as Allan."

"You *studied* him? How could you do such a thing. You were the cause of this!"

"Don't you see?" Father beseeches me. "I may have failed at finding a cure for typhus, but I created something even more powerful! The ability to separate good and evil. Just think of the possibilities. This serum can erase man's imperfections."

"So we are all to be split into two personalities?" I shake my head at his logic. I cannot fathom how he thinks such a thing should even be possible. Such callousness runs deep within him. Perhaps that is his curse as a scientist. As a physician.

"We could be stripped free of our *flaws*," he corrects me. "Imagine, pairing this cure with the technique of bringing the brain and the heart back to life. We can make—"

I interrupt him. "Father, please . . . listen to what you're saying." He looks up at me, his eyes wild. Gently,

I take the jar he still holds and place it back on the shelf. "We cannot be separated into two personalities. Look at what it has done to Allan."

"I can fix him. I swear it—"

"How can you be sure?" I cut him off. "What if you have another failure? And another, before it can be made right? Because of what you did to Allan, that other part of him—*Edgar*—set this fire. And Grand-père is dead because of it. So are the other victims of Edgar's rage. You may not have committed the physical acts, but you are surely just as responsible for their deaths as he is."

He shakes his head. "That's not so."

"It is so, Father! Why can't you see it?"

"All I'm responsible for is creating a serum. What he does because of it is not in my control."

I'm dumbfounded by Father's refusal to accept any culpability. "You gave it to him, and you keep giving it to him! Allan would not be this way if not for you."

"I stopped supplying him with the serum a week ago," Father argues. "And I did not have enough of it stored so he could keep taking it. He must have been able to replicate the process on his own."

"That may be true, but whatever he's done is

insufficient. He said you must find a way to keep him as Edgar permanently."

"Only one side can have full control. If it's going to be Edgar, then Allan shall cease to exist."

I inhale sharply. "Edgar cannot be allowed to be the one who remains. You must—"

"So it will be him, then? You've chosen." Edgar enters the room. In his hands is a flintlock pointed directly at me. "It's a poor decision, but one I cannot say is entirely unexpected."

"Turn that pistol away from my daughter, Poe," Father demands.

Edgar complies, and turns the weapon on Father. "You know what I'm after. Come now, don't make me ask again."

"I cannot give you what you seek. Your circumstances were an accident. An unknown quantity. It cannot be controlled or duplicated. The conditions would have to be exactly the same as they were before, and that is not possible. I cannot recreate it."

"That's a lie. I've already replicated the serum by using my own blood. But it doesn't last as long. I need something stronger. Something that cannot be undone."

"Allan cannot be undone!" I say. "He is your true self. You are just the side effect."

Edgar's jaw tightens. "Then why does he need me to fuel his writing? Why does he need me to fulfill his darkest urges? He's not the one in control . . . I am. And soon I won't have to wonder where he goes . . ."—he reaches out and touches a piece of my hair, letting it slide through his fingers—"or who he spends his time with."

"Get your hands off of her," Father says.

Edgar gives him a sly smile. "Acting the part of the affronted Father now, are we? My, my. What a change."

"I have always . . . cared for my daughter," Father sputters.

"Yet you thought nothing of allowing her to stay here while you continued to study me."

"I told the staff to keep her away from you! I was protecting her."

"And when news came of a murderer roaming the streets of Philadelphia?" Edgar continues. "Why did you not send her away to a safer place? When she wandered the house at night? Did you know, she was secretly meeting with me?"

My cheeks burn at his words. How he's twisted the

truth. "I came upon the library by accident one night, and he found me there. I left as soon as I was able. It was nothing more."

"Your words wound me, my dear Annabel," Edgar says. "You think so little of our time together?" He grabs my hand and rubs his thumb over the fragile skin at my wrist. "You knew it was me when you saw I had the taffy wrapper you gave to Allan. Admit it."

I pull my hand back swiftly. "I knew no such thing!" The room has grown warmer and my heart suddenly wants to beat right out of my chest.

"Enough of this," Father says. "Why don't we adjourn to the study, Edgar? We can continue our discussion there in private."

"I think we can continue this discussion right here," Edgar says. He pulls back the hammer of the flintlock, and Father's face grows pale.

"Surely, you cannot mean to shoot me, when you've gone to so much trouble to convince me to help you."

"You're right." Edgar points the weapon at me again. "I can find some . . . *other* . . . motivation to prompt you to do as I say."

I look frantically at Father.

"I cannot think with that thing so near my

daughter!" he explodes. And then I know what he's about to do.

I take a step toward him with an outstretched hand. "Father, please. You must not—"

But he moves faster than I do.

Suddenly, he's upon Edgar, and they struggle for control of the flintlock. Father tries to pry Edgar's fingers from the steel locked tightly in his grip. And Edgar's face goes red as he fights to keep his hold.

A sharp cry of pain fills the air as Father bites down on Edgar's thumb. Then there's the sound of flesh being struck and shattering glass. Father rears back with a dazed expression. A thin line of blood runs down his face.

I look down at my feet, seeing the scattered remains, and realize Edgar grabbed the glass jar off the shelf next to Father and used it to hit him. I glance desperately around for something else to hand to Father, but there's nothing.

Father stumbles. His leg threatens to buckle beneath him.

"Father, no!" I yell. I launch myself at Edgar, pushing my way in between them. *If I can just grasp the flintlock—*

But there's a pop. Something suddenly wedges itself in my chest. It feels as if I am being tied with a thousand corset laces all at once and the air has been sucked from my lungs. I stagger backward.

And fall to the ground.

Twenty-Five

I float weightlessly, somewhere high above my body. I'm no longer tied down and the feeling that I could be tumbled along by nothing more than a stray breeze is sheer bliss.

The sky is a beautiful blue, a blue I've never seen before, and I float happily along for a while until I see a shadow in the distance. It waves at me to come closer.

The shadow starts to take form, and slowly I recognize Grand-père's twinkling blue eyes and white hair. He waves again at me and I force myself down toward the ground. "Grand-père!" I shout. "Grand-père!"

The ground rushes up to meet me and though he does not speak, Grand-père returns my embrace when I run to him and hold him tightly. "I miss you," I whisper.

He pulls back, and points at something in his hand. There, nestled in the middle of his palm, is the elephant I gave him when we first met. He smiles and places it carefully in his coat pocket before he takes a step back. He takes another, and then another, until he disappears from my view.

I close my eyes, and when I open them again, an elephant and rider are on the horizon. Grand-père's snow-white hair glints in the sun, and I see he's the one riding the elephant. He begins to wave, and joy fills the cracks in my heart that were so recently filled with sorrow.

"I love you, Grand-père!" I shout again, and again, waving at him until he is just a speck on the horizon. "I miss you! I love you. . . ."

❀　❀　❀

The words are still upon my lips when I take my first breath. My chest tightens, and I feel it struggle to rise and fall. Then my scarf is pulled away and the top of my gown is loosened.

"She needs air!" a voice next to me says. "She must breathe!"

No, stop. You will reveal my scars. I don't know if I've said the words out loud or not.

Air fills my lungs again, and I try desperately to hold on to it. But the ache in my chest is strong. It wants to pull me back under.

"Annabel," an urgent voice whispers in my ear. "Come back to me, Annabel. Come back."

I know that voice. I know that voice, I know it. . . .

"There is no blood," Father says, "she should be breathing."

I struggle once more to force air into my lungs.

Slowly, painfully, the ache begins to lessen, and I open my eyes. Father is leaning over me, and Allan is holding me in his arms. My heart thumps painfully.

Allan. Not Edgar.

He touches my cheek, and I stiffen. "That is to be the way of it, then," he says. He gives me a sad smile and pulls away.

Father leans in closer to help me sit up. "I thought we had lost you. You did not breathe. . . ."

I glance around me, and realize I'm lying on the floor of the laboratory. "What happened?"

"Edgar's gun went off."

"Have I been shot? Am I dying?"

Father points to the book on the floor beside me— Mother's zodiac book—with a balled-up piece of steel in the middle of it.

I have been shot, but Mother saved me.

Taking another deep breath, I suddenly register cold air hitting my chest. My scarf is no longer around my neck. And my scars are fully visible.

Hastily pulling the edges of my dress together, I try to get to my feet. My knees threaten to buckle, but Allan catches me. "I won't let you fall."

I find myself leaning into him for just a moment, making silent wishes to myself. *I wish I did not know that a part of Allan set the fire that killed Grand-père. I wish I could un-see all the horror Edgar has shown me. I wish Father was not the one responsible for this. . . .*

I wish . . .

Taking a deep breath, I steady myself and pull away. "We will find a cure for this, Allan. I promise."

Twenty-Six

Two Weeks Later

Maddy glances furtively behind us as we slip away from the cemetery where we were supposed to have been visiting Grand-père's grave. "Hurry, Annabel," she says. "We have to get you changed. You cannot wear a dress to the men's ward."

We walk quickly, and I think of the last time we took this same path to her house. The night she woke me to come help her mother. It seems so long ago, and yet it has not been even a month.

My hand briefly touches my scarf. *How much I have changed since coming to Philadelphia. . . .*

Maddy directs me up the stairs and to the door that

leads to the flat she once shared with her brothers and sisters. I clutch the small bag I hold tightly. Within moments, she is unlacing me from my black mourning gown and helping me into the cotton pants and long-sleeved shirt that were in the bag.

A wave of homesickness washes over me as the shirt passes over my head. I have not worn these clothes since my time with Mother and the missionaries.

"Do you have the bottle?" Maddy asks. "Hide it in yer pocket until we get in."

I nod. "I took some from the jar on Father's desk and put it in a vial."

"Remember, Annabel, you must go straight there an' then come straight back to where Mama is. If we should be separated . . ." She shudders. "It's not a place you want to be lost in."

"I am well prepared, Maddy. I have memorized the corridors."

She bobs her head and then hands me a hat. "If we're stopped yer my brother Charlie," she reminds me. "Don't forget."

I tuck my long brown hair beneath the hat and give her another nod. We race back down the stairs and away from her house, fighting every second of precious time that is slowly ticking away from us. She leads me down several alleyways until we finally come to a grand stone building that bears the words PENNSYLVANIA HOSPITAL in engraved letters upon the front of it. It's so big, I can do nothing more than stare up for a moment.

Maddy nudges me. "Come along, Annabel."

I keep my head down as I follow her in through the gate and past a guard who seems to be sleeping when he ought to be keeping watch. We enter a poorly lit building with filth smeared upon the walls; and the sounds, as we travel through the corridors to reach the room where her mother is being kept, are haunting. Moans fill the air, punctuated with a slow, steady sobbing that leaves me desperately wanting to help these poor people.

Maddy must notice my anxiousness, because she grabs my hand and squeezes it. "Almost there."

I keep my eyes on the dirt-encrusted floor and keep moving beside her. When she finally comes to a halt, I look up.

"Go now, Annabel," she says urgently. "An' hurry back."

I squeeze her hand again and then release it, mentally reviewing the steps I need to take to get me to the men's ward. It's not a safe place to be, Maddy has warned me. I need to be quick in my mission.

Several steps later, I find my way and the men's ward is in front of me. Here, there are no sounds of sobbing. Only silence. Locating the third hallway, I turn down it and come to room fifty-seven. The room that Maddy told me I must find.

There are bars across the hole carved out of the wooden door to serve as a window, and I approach it carefully. It's dimly lit inside, and my eyes take some time to adjust to the bare cot lying on the floor. "Allan?" I whisper tentatively.

I can barely comprehend that he has been here these past two weeks. That he thought the only way to atone for Edgar's sins was to lock himself away in an insane asylum.

The sound of chains dragging across the floor greets me.

"Allan?" I try again. "I need to speak with you. It's urgent. I don't have much time."

A moment later, his face appears at the door. He has lost an alarming amount of weight. His cheekbones are sharp as razors. The light in his dark brown eyes has been replaced with a vacant stare that worries me.

"Allan?"

His lips part, and he whispers my name. "Annabel . . ."

"Oh, Allan." Tears fill my eyes, and I cannot stop myself. I reach my hand up to the bars. He puts a trembling finger out and touches me. "I must be quick. I cannot stay long." I cast a glance over my shoulder. "I need your help. Father has been kidnapped. We received a ransom note, but when I tried to pay it, he was not returned. I need someone to help me find him."

Reaching into my pocket, I pull out the small vial. I don't know if he will take it. Can I even ask such a thing of him? To return to the very state that put him here?

I slide my hand up to the window. I do not have a choice. *I must find a way to rescue Father.* "The serum," I say simply.

He withdraws his finger and I cast another glance behind me. My time is growing short. I need to get back to Maddy.

Then he says in a voice so soft I almost think I'm dreaming it, "What do you need?"

"Edgar." I hold the vial out to him. "I need Edgar."

Author's Note

This book is a work of fiction, but there are several real-life connections I found fascinating when I started researching the background for this story. The first is Edgar Allan Poe. So much has been written about his time in Boston, Baltimore, and New York City that, when I found the small, but significant, connection to Philadelphia, I knew it was the perfect setting.

Although "The Tell-Tale Heart" was published in 1843, "The Raven" in 1845, and "Annabel Lee" in 1849, I chose to set this story in the year 1826 to cover the "lost time" while Poe was registered at the University of Virginia. I wondered what might have happened after the semester he spent there if he had taken a position as an assistant in a medical laboratory to support himself. . . . For this story, I presumed he would have started writing some of the works I referenced much earlier than the years they were published.

Pennsylvania Hospital, the first U.S. hospital, is real and is also located in Philadelphia. (America's first surgical amphitheater and America's first medical library are located on the second and third floors of the historic Pine Building of the hospital. I highly recommend you visit them both if you get the chance.)

Annabel's hero, Dr. Elizabeth Blackwell, was the first woman physician in the United States. She, too, has a connection to Philadelphia, although I have taken poetic license with two pieces of her history: The first was advancing her timeline by twenty years. Dr. Blackwell was only five years old in 1826. The second was having her achieve her lifelong goal of becoming a surgeon. Due to an eye infection that caused her to lose sight in her left eye, Dr. Blackwell was never able to attain this position. It only felt right in my world to make that dream come true.

As for the Washington Irving reference? Edgar Allan Poe was indeed aware of, and corresponded with, Washington Irving.

Acknowledgments

Great big heaps of thanks to Mollie, fab assistant Katie, and the rest of the team at Foundry Literary + Media for seeing this project off the ground and steering the ship.

Even bigger heaps of thanks to my amazing and wonderful editor, Alison, who knew how to wield those track changes of magic, when to talk me down from the ledge, let me make those last-LAST minute edits, and always remembers how much she loves me when I bring up the dreaded, "So, about that deadline . . ." topic of conversation.

To the Egmont team—Margaret and Michelle and Regina and anyone else I may have forgotten (I'm sorry! I love you! Still friends?)—thank you for your tremendous support and enthusiasm and contagious good cheer. Working on this project with you has been one of the best things ever.

Thank you, dear readers, for seeing me through another one. (Yes, there IS a sequel. Don't worry! I won't leave you hanging.) You have a million choices out there, and any time you choose to read my words, it leaves me thrilled and honored and so very happy. Thank you.

Friends and family, your continued support and love means the world to me. There is no thank-you I can say that is big enough to cover it all.

Lorrie and Lauren—thank you for always knowing what to say and how to say it. May your kindness and generosity be returned x3. Love you guys!

And finally, all my love and thanks to Lee—my rock, my rope-climbing partner, my everything. *Amor Vincit Omnia*

Works Referenced

"Annabel Lee" by Edgar Allan Poe. First published in the *New-York Daily Tribune*, October 9, 1849.

"The Mask of the Red Death" by Edgar Allan Poe. First published in *Graham's Magazine*, May 1842.

"The Raven" by Edgar Allan Poe. First published in the *Evening Mirror*, January 29, 1845.

"The Tell-Tale Heart" by Edgar Allan Poe. First published in the *Pioneer*, January 1843.

Strange Case of Dr. Jekyll and Mr. Hyde by Robert Louis Stevenson. London: *Longmans, Green, & Co.*, 1886.